RAVE REVIEWS
FOR T.M. WRIGIIT!

"T. M. Wright has a unique imagination."

—Dean Koontz

"T. M. Wright is a master of the subtle fright that catches you by surprise and never quite lets you go. He is one of the finest modern interpreters of the ghost story."

—Whitley Strieber

"Wright convincingly proves that he understands, as few do, how to give a scare without spilling blood all over the page."

—*Publishers Weekly*

"T. M. Wright is one of the best ghost story writers around."

—*American Fantasy*

"I have been an unabashed fan of T. M. Wright's since reading his first novel."

—Charles L. Grant

"T. M. Wright is a brilliant writer. His impeccable prose is hypnotic and the rhythm of his words entrancing."

—*2 A.M. Magazine*

"Keep an eye on T. M. Wright."

—*The Philadelphia Inquirer*

"Wright's slow escalation of terror is masterly."

—*The Sun Times* (U.K.)

"Nobody docs ghosts better than T. M. Wright."

—Kim Newman

T. M. WRIGHT
Sleepeasy

LEISURE BOOKS NEW YORK CITY

A LEISURE BOOK®

April 2001

Published by

Dorchester Publishing Co., Inc.
276 Fifth Avenue
New York, NY 10001

ISBN 0-8439-4864-7

The name "Leisure Books" and the stylized "L" with design are trademarks of Dorchester Publishing Co., Inc.

Printed in the United States of America.

Visit us on the web at www.dorchesterpub.com.

For Mary Anne, with love

Sleepeasy

Chapter One

These were the last words that Harry Briggs uttered in this life: "Hey, you! What in the hell do you think you're doing?"

He was calling to a craggy-faced, red-haired man standing not far off, in a field of new snow. The man didn't answer him.

The last living thing that Harry Briggs saw was his wife, naked and beautiful, rising into the air as she prepared to dive.

Harry had thought more than once of shucking his career as a professor of philosophy and doing something completely different. What did philosophy have to offer anyway? Only lots of unanswerable questions. What did anyone need with unanswerable questions? They only made life more difficult. Who the hell cared about Camus and Kierkegaard and Sartre anymore, except his students, who *had* to care about them if they wanted a passing grade. The answer to the question of humanity's existence on the earth was simple—people were put here to enjoy themselves. To smell the heady aromas of salt air and pine forests, to make love when and where the urge struck and to eat themselves into oblivion. *Living* equaled hedonism. Philosophically, Harry knew it was so. But putting that philosophy completely into practice was impossible for him.

The last film that Harry saw in this life was *The Maltese Falcon*. It was one of his favorites; along with *The Big Sleep, Trouble in Mind* and *Chinatown*. He liked detective films because he thought their heroes were ballsy, no-shit kinds of guys, and that was the kind of guy he had always wanted to be. A 1940s kind of guy. The kind of guy who used words like "buddy," "Java" and "gams," and who called attractive women "hot numbers" or "classy dames." The kind of guy who, beneath this gruff, absurd and anachronistic exterior, was single-mindedly on the side of *good*. Harry wanted to be single-minded.

His last meal in this life was potatoes au gratin and ham.

His last conversation was with his wife, Barbara, shortly before she went for one of her nude swims. Their conversation was, ironically, about death and dying, about being dead and what came *afterward*. Barbara maintained that it would be peachy if, afterward, after death, everyone had a chance to create their own private universe, complete with their own kinds of people and their own kinds of houses, and smells and sensations, *et cetera*. A place where wishes were made real. A place, and people, as easily molded as wet clay. Harry conceded that this would be wonderful, but he doubted that *anything* happened after death.

"It's just not in the cards," he said.

"And how would you know?" Barbara said.

Harry shrugged. "I guess I wouldn't," he conceded, because he was always on the lookout for a fight brewing and always wary of participating in one.

Barbara pursed her lips. She was an exquisitely beautiful woman, he thought. She was even beautiful when she was pursing her lips.

"C'mon, Harry, don't be such a wimp," she said. "Give me an argument, for Christ's sake."

There were a couple of reasons that Harry didn't want to give Barbara an argument. Most importantly, she was right: how would he know, indeed, what happened after death (and, for that matter, how would *she* know?)? Secondly, if he got into a long, philosophical discussion with her, she would delay her nude swim, and that would be a pity, because the longer she delayed it, the more likely she would be to simply not do it. The hour was late, after all. And it was Christmas Eve, so, even though the pool was heated, the air wasn't.

Harry shook his head. "No, you're right, darling. I really wouldn't know anything about what happens after death. No one would."

"Including me?"

He shrugged again. "Well, sure."

"You just want me to get naked, don't you, Harry?"

He grinned, then fought the grin back because it was not, after all, the way a ballsy, no-shit guy reacted to such a question. "We'll both get naked," he said, stone-faced.

"Oh? And what are you going to do once you're naked?"

He said nothing for a moment, then answered, "Swim, I guess."

"Swim?" She smiled. "Harry, the act of swimming requires that you actually get into the water."

"Sure, I know that. Of course."

She sighed. "Keep your clothes on, Harry. Just watch me. I don't want you stepping out of character."

Harry's last dessert in this life was muskmelon and strawberries with whipped cream. It was one of his favorites.

The last book he read was *Jurassic Park*, which he thought was entertaining but preposterous.

And his last coherent thought in this life was, *Barbara? Is this a joke?*

Afterward

Chapter Two

Harry had been driving for a long time on a road that seemed to snake endlessly through fields of tall grass and nodding sunflowers. He wasn't sure how long he'd been driving. It felt like centuries. He'd stopped for coffee and for meals—at friendly little restaurants that rose up magically from the fields of tall grass and sunflowers—and he'd stopped to stretch his legs, but he hadn't stopped to sleep and he thought that he should be getting tired by now. He supposed that it was midafternoon when he decided this, and that he was sweating because the road that cut through the nodding sunflowers and tall grass was supernaturally hot.

He didn't notice until the deed was done that a fat, black spider had crawled up from somewhere inside the car's front seat and bitten him on his bare forearm. He saw the spider—it was staring at him with tiny red eyes—and he saw the slight discolored area on his arm, so he hit the brake pedal and pulled over to the shoulder of the road.

"Jesus," he whispered, not because the bite hurt, but because it was so unsettling to be bitten and not have noticed right away. It was unsettling also to have huge black spiders living inside his car's front seat. There might be dozens of spiders in there. Aunt and uncle spiders, mother and father spiders, baby spiders waiting to grow up. A whole community of fat spiders with tiny red eyes.

He stared at the spider that was staring at him from his bare forearm—gripping the steering wheel—and he realized that he didn't know what to do. He thought that the spider had to be killed, of course. If he didn't kill it, it would bite him again, and who knew what kind of spider it was and what the effects of its bite might be? But if he slapped it with his other hand, it might bite him again, then and there. And if he tried to shake it off, it might bite him too, because it was clinging to him with legs that looked as big as pencils.

Perhaps the spider was cold inside the car's front seat, although that seemed unlikely on such a hot day. Or perhaps it merely wanted light and air. Blood and companionship. So it had staked a claim to his forearm, and if he, Harry, tried to uproot it, it would probably bite him again.

"You can't stay there," Harry said, and the creature moved its huge front legs a little, as if in response.

At last, it lumbered off, down his forearm and into the seat again. Harry thought it was amazing that a spider so big could slip through the crack between the seat bottom and the seat back.

When he looked up again, he saw that the shadows

had lengthened and that dusk, like a shower of fire, was upon him.

Harry showed a photograph to a woman behind the counter at a natural foods store called Sustenance for the Spirit and asked if she had ever seen the person in the photograph. The woman answered that she hadn't, then added, "But there are so many people coming and going these days. It's like a parade," which confused Harry, who hadn't seen another soul on the road all day. He nodded, frowned, said, "Thanks, anyway," and bought some of the woman's natural foods, because he felt duty-bound to now that he had taken up her time.

When he was putting the groceries in his car, he noticed that the spot where the spider had bitten him had swollen alarmingly to the size of a Ping-Pong ball. He decided that this was okay, however, because the arm didn't hurt, or itch, and he was feeling all right otherwise.

He stopped at a gas station and showed the man tending the pumps the same photograph. The man looked at it for a moment and said, "She's one classy dame, ain't she?" Harry agreed, but then the man went on to say that he had never seen her before and that even if he had, he probably wouldn't remember her, considering how "crowded the roads have been." Harry frowned, said thanks, put $5 worth of gasoline into his monster Buick—though he didn't need the gasoline—and drove off.

It was well past dark when Harry remembered that he was probably tired. He began looking for motels. Within a half hour, he passed several that had NO VACANCY signs out—one sign read NO VACANCY, NO NOTHIN', KEEP MOVING! in big, blue neon letters, which Harry thought very strange indeed. He passed one that had a vacancy, but its parking lot was too brightly lit and he thought he would never get to sleep with so much light coming in through the curtains. Then he pulled into a motel called Habuda's Heavenly Hideaway, which had a dark parking lot and only a green neon OPEN sign at its office door.

He showed the man behind the counter the same photograph as before and asked, "You seen her, buddy? I'm looking for her," and noted that this was the first time he had ever called another man "buddy." He liked it. It was straightforward, it was no-shit.

The man—short, dark-haired and chunky—studied the photograph for a few seconds, handed it back, and shook his head. "Sorry, no," he said. "I have not seen her. Is she missing?"

Harry nodded and put the photograph back into his shirt pocket. "Sure, yeah," he said gruffly, "missing." He paused, then added, with a little catch in his voice, "I know that *I* miss her," which elicited a curious look from the chunky man, who then asked Harry to fill out the motel's registration form.

As Harry did this, he noticed that his arm was still swollen where the spider had bitten him, and that it was beginning to turn several gaudy shades of purple too.

"That looks like a nasty bite," said the man behind the counter.

"I think it probably looks worse than it really is," Harry replied. He finished filling out the form, got his keys and said gruffly, "Ain't nothin'. No pain," before going to his room.

As he lay on his bed in his clothes in the darkened motel room—only a sliver of green light shone beneath the bottom of the curtain on the picture window—Harry thought about his wife and wondered if, at that moment, she was thinking of him. How could it be otherwise? he decided. They had shared so much. They shared so much even now. His life was her life and her life was his life. They *were* each other. How many relationships grew to be that wonderfully close? Only a lucky few.

> *"Do you ever do this, Barbara? Do you ever stop and think that someday, far in the future, the person you're living with, the person you're sharing space with on the earth, is going to be gone . . ."*
>
> *"You mean dead?"*
>
> *"Dead. Sure. Gone. And when you stop and think about it, you think that it simply won't happen. This person who shares your life can't possibly stop sharing it with you. And you can't possibly stop sharing your life with her."*
>
> *"You mean me?"*
>
> *"Of course you. Who else?"*
>
> *"I appreciate your devotion, Harry."*
>
> *" 'Appreciate' it?"*
>
> *"Yes. It's very sweet. I appreciate it."*

He remembered eating with her. They ate the same things, almost completely shared the same tastes. Asparagus, potatoes au gratin, fettucini alfredo, strawberries and cream, burritos, enchiladas and Swedish meatballs.

It is so good, Harry decided, to eat tasty food with someone who finds the same food tasty.

Their favorite restaurant had been a place called

Wanda's, and Harry didn't know if it still existed. It could have been torn down, burned, closed, sold. Things in life changed so quickly. What was there to count on or cling to? Only memories. Only the past.

The present, so fleeting and so mercurial, twisted this way and that because of the past, and danced to the tune that the past sang.

He got out of bed to pee. He stood over the toilet in the brightly lit bathroom for a long time, but, though the urge was strong, nothing happened. Harry found this very frustrating.

He stared at the swelling on his arm and decided that it was nothing to worry about. It looked awful, but then so did a bruise. So did a black eye. And bruises and black eyes were nothing to worry about.

He went back to bed. The urge to pee had left him completely.

When he thought about his wife, he found that he couldn't remember the color of her hair. He could remember her smell, her laugh, the size and shape of her nipples, the color of her eyes, the way she ate—with gusto—the way she made love, the way she pouted, the way she chided him for small misdeeds. But he couldn't remember the color of her hair, and that wasn't good. Certainly he should be able to remember the color of his wife's hair. They had shared so many years, so much tasty food. If he couldn't remember the color of her hair, then there was something wrong with him.

He fingered the photograph in his shirt pocket. But what could it tell him? he wondered. It was a black and white photograph. And how would he be able to see it in the dark anyway?

He decided that remembering his wife's hair color wasn't important. Remembering her voice, her words, the ache she created in him—these were more important things.

"*Are you happy?*"
" *'Happy'? That's a sloshy sort of word.*"
"*I mean with me. Are you happy with me?*"
"*Even that particular sentiment is sloshy.*
We have our own lives to live, after all, so the
idea of being happy 'with' someone is not
very instructive, is it?"
"*You're playing games again.*"
"*Am I?*"

He got out of bed and went to the motel office. No one was there. Only one dim light was on and, in combination with the green neon OPEN sign on the outside of the glass door, it lit the small room badly.

He found a bell on the front desk and rang it. It was as loud as a church bell.

The motel's proprietor appeared from a back room. He had apparently been eating, because he was wiping his mouth with a napkin. He politely asked what Harry wanted and Harry asked, "Is there a restaurant nearby?"

"We have a little restaurant here," the proprietor answered, "but it's not open now. Not enough people are staying to open it."

"What are you talking about, buddy?" Harry said, and grinned quickly. "I was told that there were all kinds of people passing by."

The proprietor smiled. "We are off the beaten path, I'm afraid."

"Sure," Harry said. "I was just looking for a cup of java." He went back to his room, took off his clothes and got under the blankets.

His search was futile. No one anywhere knew what he really wanted.

He closed his eyes and thought about his wife: about the size and shape of her nipples, about her voice and her smell, about tasty food. . . .

Spaces in the Emptiness

Chapter Three

As he struggled through the dark water, toward the pinpoint of yellow light so terribly far above him, Sam Goodlow, former private investigator, thought that he must be sinking. Inhaling brine and becoming light-headed and giddy. Thinking odd thoughts about naked women he wished he had known.

God, God, the water was closing in. He wanted to scream, but who could scream at a time like this?

And who was he anyway? How had he gotten into this precarious position? When would his lungs explode? And when they did, would the end come quickly and silently? Instant oblivion? A moment's unease, then nothing? Who could hope for more? Or less?

He wondered why it was taking so long. The tiny point of yellow light above was growing smaller as he struggled up through the dark water, which meant, surely, that he was sinking, that his lungs were filling up and his belly was bloating with brine, that the flesh eaters of the sea were gathering around, waiting for the explosive moment—the sprinkling of fleshy Goodlow bits through the dark lake, their watery evening's heady repast.

The water was so cold. Death was so cold. Panic and dying were such cold and anxious things.

Perhaps he should have worn a sweater.

Chapter Four

When Harry arrived in Silver Lake he was wearing a rumpled brown trench coat over a threadbare, double-breasted gray suit. He also carried a snub-nosed .38 in a shoulder holster whose tight leather strap chafed him, so he was constantly rearranging it. A black fedora lay on the seat beside him. He glanced at it as he turned off his monster Buick's ignition. Did he have the chutzpah to wear the fedora? he wondered. He wasn't sure. He left it on the seat.

Dusk was about to fall. No one was around except a woman sitting on a park bench. She had her back to him and was apparently looking at the lake.

"The place is deserted," he said out loud, hoping that he wasn't taking her by surprise. "Where the hell is everyone?"

"In the lake," she answered, without turning her head toward him.

She looked comfortable. Her legs were crossed, her

face was tilted into the fading light, her bare arms rested on the top of the bench. Her auburn hair was down to her shoulders and her arms and legs had a good, even tan. Nice gams, Harry thought. She's a hot number.

"Everyone's swimming?" he asked.

She nodded.

"But I don't see anyone."

She lifted her arm slightly and pointed to the other side of the small lake. Dusk had turned the water a tarnished silver, though it should have been rust-colored. "There's a beach," she said. "See it?"

He looked. The lake seemed to be barely a mile across and if there had been a beach, he would have seen it, he thought. But he saw only a narrow band of green, probably a line of trees that were lush with summer foliage. "No," he said. "I don't see it."

She let her arm drop. "It's there. It's very small." She looked at him. She was wearing sunglasses, but because of the slant of daylight, he could see that her eyes were brown. He thought he had seen those eyes before.

She gave him a quick once-over and grinned. "What are *you* supposed to be?" she asked.

The question took him aback. Wasn't it clear what he was supposed to be?

She went on, "Aren't you hot in that trench coat?"

He shook his head. "I don't get hot. I don't get cold either." What was he saying?

She grinned again. "Really? That's quite a talent."

"Yeah," he said. "It's a wild talent." He shoved his hands deep into the pockets of his trench coat. The shoulder holster strap was chafing again, but he tried to ignore it. "My name's Harry Briggs," he said gruffly. "I'm looking for someone. I'm looking for a woman."

"Is that right?"

He nodded once, briskly. "Yeah, that's right."

"And just who is it you're looking for, Mr. Briggs?" She smiled a little, as if at a private joke.

Harry took the black and white snapshot out of his pocket and handed it over. "I'm looking for her."

The woman glanced at the photograph, smiled—again as if at a private joke—and handed it back. "Who is she?"

"Who is she?"

"Yes. What's her name?"

Harry wondered how candid he should be. He mistrusted this woman. He wasn't sure why. It was almost instinctive. He got the discomforting idea that she was playing games with him. "Babs," he said.

"Babs? What an old-fashioned name. It's a very 1940s kind of name, isn't it?"

"I'm a 1940s kind of guy."

She nodded. "Of course you are, Mr. Briggs." She paused, then said, "Babs? That's short for Barbara, isn't it?"

"Yeah, sure. I guess it is."

"Babs, then." Another smile. "I'll go along with that. She's *your* missing person, after all."

He didn't like her tone. "Listen, sister," he barked, "what I'd appreciate here is some cooperation. This is serious business."

"Of course it is." She grinned.

"And what I don't want is a lot of bullshit!"

"I didn't realize that that was what I was giving you, Mr. Briggs. I apologize."

29

He said nothing. He was surprised, and a little embarrassed, by his outburst.

"Mr. Briggs," she said, "do you think that I'm a nun?"

"Huh?"

"You called me 'sister,' so clearly you believe I'm a nun." She paused. "I am most definitely *not* a nun."

He shrugged. "No, I don't think you're a nun. It was merely a term of salutation . . ."

"Salutation. Of course." She grinned again.

"Sure. Like 'buddy,' or 'mister.' If you don't like it, I won't use it."

"That would be nice."

He looked silently at her for a moment. She was a very combative person and he wasn't sure what he thought of that.

He sat down next to her. The park bench rested on a gray concrete slab ten feet above the shoreline and there were several boat docks below. One of them held a red canoe, the others were empty. "Hell," he chirped, trying to strike an apologetic tone, "you don't *look* like a nun."

"I'll take that as a compliment."

"It was meant to be one." He turned his gaze to the silver lake and went on, "Okay, I'll tell you the truth." It was a lie. "I'm doing someone a favor." He noticed that she smelled slightly of baby oil. "I'm here to do a friend a favor." He leaned forward so his elbows were on his knees and his hands were clasped. Suddenly he felt like talking. This was something new for him. The only people he'd ever felt like talking to—opening up to—before had been his mother, a younger cousin and Barbara. He decided that it wouldn't be wise to indulge this urge

30

to talk. It would also be very much out of character—out of character, at any rate, for a man in a
trench coat and shoulder holster. He hurried on,
though, unable to stop.

"That's why friends exist, isn't it? So we can do
favors for them. When one friend says to another, for
instance, 'Hey, I like your new haircut,' it's a favor,
even if the haircut is lousy." He grinned. "Because
hair grows back, doesn't it? It's not something someone would say to a stranger. He'd say instead, 'Got
a new haircut, huh?' Or we read a friend's short story
and tell him it's good, or we put an arm around his
shoulder when his cat dies, although we've avoided
such physical contact before."

He glanced at her and she smiled back. He liked
her smile now. It was a familiar sort of smile. "I'm
sorry," he said. "I'm talking too much." He became
stone-faced. "I don't usually." He looked at the lake
once more. Its bright silver surface seemed illusory.
He could have been looking at a mirage.

"I get it," she said. "You're supposed to be a detective, right?"

He nodded slowly. "Actually, miss, I'm a PI."

"Of course you are," she said. "A PI." The whole
exchange seemed to be tickling her. "A private
dick."

"Yeah," he whispered hoarsely. "Private dick." He
reached inside the trench coat to readjust his shoulder
holster. Maybe talcum powder would help the chafing, he thought. His fingers touched the cross-hatched
grip of the snub-nosed .38. The gun felt heavy, alien,
obscene.

"My name's Amelia," the woman said. "And if you
want to talk to me about this woman you're looking
for, that's fine."

31

Harry saw that her gaze was on the lake again, that her arms were still on the back of the park bench, her smooth, tanned legs still crossed. She wore a white, sleeveless shirt and white shorts, which set off her tan nicely. He stared at her for a few moments, hoping she'd look at him again, but she didn't.

"I'm a kind of friend of this woman I'm looking for."

"A friend of Babs-slash-Barbara, you mean?"

"Yeah. That's what I mean."

"And I'd say you were a very good friend, Harry, to have come so far."

"How do you know how far I've come?" he asked.

She inclined her head toward the monster Buick and answered, "Your license plates."

"Oh. Well, actually, I know her husband and he hired me to come down here and find her."

"And bring her back?"

"If that's what she wants."

"Then you really are a detective?"

He nodded. "It's actually a second profession. I used to . . . teach."

"English?"

"Philosophy."

"Camus, Kierkegaard, Sartre?"

He nodded glumly. "Uh-huh. But they didn't teach me nothin'."

"So you don't teach anymore?"

He shook his head and answered tersely, "I investigate."

"Missing people?"

"That's right."

"Like . . . Babs?"

"That's right."

"Judging from her photograph, Mr. Briggs, I'd say she's a beautiful woman. Does the photograph do her justice?"

"Not really. She's a real hot number. A classy dame."

"And a very lucky dame to have as capable a man as you looking for her."

"That's what friends are for, miss."

"You can call me Amelia."

"Sure. Amelia."

She looked at the lake again.

Harry looked too. It was a darker silver now, nearly gray, no longer illusory. It looked like cement—he thought he could have walked on it—like the sad gray slab he and the woman were sitting on.

Amelia said, "Isn't this a lovely spot? I come here almost every night. Sometimes I get in my party boat and go to the other side just before the day ends. The shoreline here looks like it's on fire when the day ends."

"*Do* you know Babs?" he asked.

She looked briefly at him, then at the lake again. "Of course I do, Harry. Everyone here knows her."

"When I was a child I dreamed about growing up and going off to college and . . ."
   "When I was a child I used to get card-board boxes and make little houses out of them. I'd cut holes for windows and tape the flaps up for the roofs and I'd get all my dolls—I had a couple dozen dolls—and I'd pretend that they lived in these houses and I was the one they were answerable to. Because I'd put them there, of course. I could make them say and do and be precisely what I wanted. They

were so malleable. They were like clay."

"You wanted to be in control, huh?"

"Of course. Don't all children want to be in control?"

Chapter Five

Sam Goodlow had never liked being a stranger. It was a cold and anxious thing to be. Strangers engendered unease, and he wanted to engender warmth, good feeling, kisses.

"Hello," he said to the naked woman, and she turned her head and smiled at him, but then turned her head away and said nothing.

He had seen this woman before, he realized. He didn't know her. But he'd seen her. Why was she being so coy?

He said hello once more, but with the same results.

He wanted to kiss her, fondle her, be a *part* of her, because she looked so warm and soft (and wasn't warmth and softness anathema to what existed everywhere else in the universe, and wasn't that what made it so tempting and good?). He stood, made his way across the grass to her, and cupped her butt cheeks in his big hands.

"I'd like to swim," she said.

He told her his name, but she didn't tell him hers, and he thought that he didn't need to know it anyway.

"I'd like to swim," she said again. She wasn't looking at him. "You should see me dive!" she added, and still she wasn't looking at him.

And he thought that he *had* seen her dive, but that it had gone badly.

She remained as still as ice and he felt that he had intruded upon her, was a stranger. And he felt that it was this too—his strangeness—that was engendering her coldness toward him, and was making her no more alive than he was, though her butt cheeks were warmer than his hands, and she smelled of sweat and baby oil and blood.

Chapter Six

Amelia stood, went gracefully down a flight of cement steps to the narrow beach and disappeared behind dense underbrush that crowded the shoreline.

Harry saw her again a minute later. She was piloting a small, gaily colored, flat-bottomed party boat toward the opposite shore. She waved casually at him and he waved back. "Welcome to Silver Lake, Harry," she called, and he watched until she and her colorful boat were lost in the quickly gathering dusk.

When he'd arrived in the little community, finding a parking space had been difficult. The Buick was as big as a tank and the roadways in Silver Lake weren't designed for such beasts. The other cars he'd seen were small. He had also noticed a few bicycles and several motorcycles, though these, like the cars, looked as if they were in various stages of disrepair.

When he had found a parking lot, he'd had to use

two spaces, otherwise the Buick's rear end would have blocked the roadway.

He got into the Buick now, started the engine and turned on the headlights. They illuminated the park bench that he and Amelia had shared and, for a moment, he thought he saw her sitting there again, her arms up and her head thrown back slightly. But, he decided, this was only an illusion.

The white sail of a boat coming in lay in his line of sight, through the slats of the bench. He decided to wait for it to dock so he could talk with its owners.

The owners were a couple in their early sixties, very fit-looking, dressed nattily for sailing and they smiled almost constantly. As they talked, an arc lamp above cast a hard green light. It seemed, from where Harry stood, to be the only street lamp burning in the community. It illuminated them, the cement slab and park bench, and fifty or sixty feet of the narrow beach and boat dock area. The silver gunwales of the red canoe caught the light, and Harry had to turn his head to avoid this harsh reflection as he talked with the old couple.

The man repeated what Harry had already heard from Amelia: "Certainly we know Babs."

The old man's wife nodded enthusiastically. "Babs is a very pleasant person, Mr. Briggs. Everyone likes her."

"Sure," he said. "She's a classy dame."

"As classy as they come," said the old woman, smiling.

"You know, son," said the old man, "I haven't heard that phrase in years. It's rather archaic, you know."

Harry shrugged. "Yeah, sure. I know . . ."

"It takes me back. I used to talk like that myself once."

Harry was growing very uncomfortable. The shoulder holster was chafing him, these people were apparently amused by him, Amelia was hiding something from him and his search for Barbara had gotten off to a very uneven start.

He asked, "Do you have any idea where Babs might be staying?"

"You mean, 'Where is she shacked up?' " said the old man, smiling toothily.

The old woman answered, "Well, I'll tell you, young man, she was staying with the Alexanders, but they're no longer with us and I haven't seen her for a few weeks. I used to see her here, in fact. She liked to—"

"Aren't you hot in that trench coat?" interrupted the woman's husband.

"No," Harry answered tersely. "I don't get hot."

"Really?" said the old man. "How interesting." He was bubbling with enthusiasm. "I'd be hotter than a chilli pepper in a frying pan. I'd be hotter than a twenty-year-old sailor in Tijuana, hotter than a cat in heat in Haiti. Mr. Briggs, your trench coat and gun are very, very diverting."

"Gun?" Harry asked.

"The bulge is obvious," said the old woman.

"Either it's a gun or you're just happy to see us," said her husband. "But, of course, your genitals would have to be sticking out of your rib cage, wouldn't they?" The old man was enjoying himself immensely.

"As I was saying," chimed in the old woman, "Babs used to like to come here and look at the lake. All by herself, I mean—when the rest of the community was on the other side." She paused. "She was a loner, Mr. Briggs, just like you." She grinned the way Amelia had, as if at some private joke.

"Not good to be a loner," the woman's husband said, smiling. "Indeed, look at us. Are we alone? No. We're together!"

"Yes," Harry said, and then didn't know how to go on. These two were a very odd pair indeed.

The woman asked, "Where are you staying, Mr. Briggs?"

Harry moved his hand a little. "A motel."

"And you've come to our little community specifically to look for Babs?" she continued, incredulously.

Harry nodded. "Yes. Her husband asked me to come here."

"What a friendly gesture," she said. "Doing her husband a favor." She paused, then said, "It's a wonderful gesture, Mr. Briggs. Perhaps you are not as alone as you believe."

Her husband turned his head briefly toward the lake and said, "The others will be returning soon. Perhaps they can be more useful." He paused, looking back at the lake. "But Gilly and I have an early day tomorrow, so you'll have to excuse us." He leaned closer, as if to speak to Harry in confidence. "Your private eye schtick, Mr. Briggs, is very entertaining, but I think you may be overdoing it a tad. Loosen up. Private eyes aren't made of stone, you know. Look at Mike Hammer, Sam Spade. They're as human as any of us."

With that, he and his wife hurried off down a little dead-end street that ran parallel to the lake shore and, like Amelia, were lost in the darkness.

Amelia's People

Chapter Seven

The street lamps in the community blinked on with the arrival of the inhabitants of Silver Lake at the beach and boat docks. Green arc lights lit up everywhere, transforming the darkness into a bizarre kind of daylight. The people themselves—half a hundred of them—were odd to look at in this harsh light. Most of them were dressed in swimsuits, though some had apparently changed into their street clothes, and their skin looked as green as summer grass. Harry looked at his own hand. It had the same cast.

He waited on the cement slab, in front of the park bench, as people docked their boats, gathered up their little tote bags and polystyrene beer coolers, their towels and inner tubes and swim fins. They seemed very animated—talkative and happy. As he waited, laughter sporadically erupted from various parts of the group. Several people who noticed him nodded and smiled. They didn't seem at all suspicious of the stranger in their midst, and this, oddly, made Harry a little uncomfortable.

He centered on a dark-haired woman who looked to be in her mid-thirties and shouted, "I'm looking for a someone named Babs."

A young man dressed in dark green shorts and a yellow short-sleeved shirt came up the cement steps. "I think that Babs is still on the other side," he said.

"You mean at the beach?" Harry asked.

The man nodded. "Uh-huh. That's where I saw her last. Sometimes she likes to simply look out at the lake. All by herself. Thinking, I guess. A real dreamer. But then, we all need to dream, Mr. Briggs."

Harry nodded vaguely at his, pulled the photograph from the breast pocket of his gray suit, handed it to the young man and asked, "Is this the woman you're talking about?"

The man looked quickly at the photograph, handed it back, then nodded again. "Yes, that's Babs."

"How did you know my name?" Harry asked.

The man smiled apologetically. "Amelia told us. We saw her on our way here. She tells us everything." He offered his hand. Harry shook it. "Welcome to Silver Lake," the man said, let go of his hand and walked off. Harry watched for a few moments as the man climbed a very narrow alley that lay at right angles to the dead-end street. Like many streets in the community, it sloped severely, so the man had to walk stooped forward to keep his balance.

"You should have joined us," Harry heard someone call from behind him. He turned. A tall, square-jawed, athletic-looking man with short blond hair, dressed only in olive-colored Speedos, strode briskly forward and offered his hand. Harry took it. The man's grip was very firm and Harry got the idea that he was relishing this little test of strength.

The man said, "If you're looking for Babs, I think you'll find her on the other side. She stays there sometimes." He smiled. His teeth were straight and whitish green under the arc lamps.

Other people gathered around. Some appeared to be on their way home, some were apparently interested in what Harry was doing there.

Harry said, "I was told that she wasn't here anymore."

"Who told you that?" the man asked.

"An old couple," Harry answered, and nodded to indicate the dead-end street. He could see now that there were half a dozen small cottages on it. "They live down there, I think. They said that Babs was staying with the Alexanders, but that the Alexanders don't live here anymore."

"Actually, we do," someone said behind the man in the Speedos. A face appeared near his shoulder. It was pleasant and smiling—the face of a woman in her fifties—and it was fringed by silver hair tinged green by the arc lights. "My name's June," she said. "You must be Mr. Briggs. Amelia told us about you. I would say that if you're looking for Babs, then you should go to the other side. She stays there sometimes. Can't decide which *side* she's on, I think. Gets sad. Gets blue. Just like you." She grinned. "Goodness, that rhymes," she went on happily. "But that's where you might find her. On the other side."

"Yes," said the man in the Speedos, glancing at her. "I told him all that."

"Thanks," Harry said, and shrugged. "But I'm afraid I have no way over there."

"Mr. Briggs," June Alexander said, "you're more

45

than welcome to use any of the boats. They're community property. I would suggest, however, that if you use one of the power boats, you leave a dollar or two for gas money in the collection can nailed to the pole. You'll see it." She offered her hand. "It was very nice meeting you. Be careful crossing now." She smiled before continuing, "If you do go out on the lake, Mr. Briggs, I'd strongly suggest taking off the trench coat. My guess is that you'll sink like a stone in it." Then she walked off, merging with the crowd.

"Yes," echoed the man in the Speedos. "Please do be careful. The lake's not very large, but these awful lights"—he looked up briefly at them—"are the only source of guidance across it now, and it's frighteningly easy to become disoriented. Sky, land and water seem to merge, and eventually you begin to feel that you're simply . . . floating." He gave Harry an odd, lopsided grin. "It's very disconcerting, Mr. Briggs. You can't imagine."

"Harry."

"Hirsute," the man said.

"Hirsute?"

"My little joke. Hirsute, as I'm sure you know, *means* hairy!"

Harry nodded. "Sure." He forced a small chuckle, though it made him feel like an ass.

The man said, "And my name's Leonard." He shook Harry's hand again, even harder this time. "Good to meet you, Hirsute." He smiled, added, "Don't be such a stranger"—which Harry thought was an odd thing to say—and then merged with the crowd.

"Leonard?" Harry called.

"Yes?"

"Can I use *any* of the boats?"

"Your choice. Oh, and, Hirsute?"

Harry grimaced and looked in the direction of Leonard's voice. He saw him standing near the monster Buick. He was pointing at the headlights, which Harry had accidentally left on.

"You'll wear your battery down," Leonard called.

"Could you turn them off?" Harry shouted back. "The door's unlocked."

Leonard nodded, then bent over, so he was peering directly into the headlight for a moment, as if the light fascinated him.

This is very odd, Harry thought.

Then Leonard straightened, went to the driver's door, opened it, reached in and turned off the headlights.

A minute later, the cement slab was empty of people and Harry was trying to decide if he really wanted to go out on Silver Lake in the dark.

"My name is Marlowe."

"It is?"

"This is a game. I'm playing a game."

"Oh. Yes. A game."

"If you can play games, why can't I?"

"Sure. Okay. You're Philip Marlowe."

"Why are your lights out, Phil?"

"No electricity. Didn't pay the bill. But who needs electricity? As long as we have lust, we have light, and heat." He slapped the mattress.

"Do you have a kerosene lamp or something?"

"Who needs lamps in bed?"

"No one, I guess."

"I want us to make love."

47

"You do?"

"Yes. Very much."

"Very much? That's disappointing."

"Why is it disappointing?"

"You're not a good games player. You just don't have the imagination for it."

"Oh?"

"And no, I don't want to make love. I don't even want to fuck, which would have been preferable."

"Why?"

"Why what? Be specific. You're so ambiguous."

"Why don't you want to fuck?"

"Some other night, okay? I'm going to take a dip in the pool."

Chapter Eight

Harry didn't swim well. His parents had made him take swimming lessons from the time he could walk until he started high school, so he had learned a number of strokes—Australian crawl, breaststroke, backstroke. But he did none of them well because he was afraid of water that was deeper than his nose. He came close to panic, though he wasn't sure why. His mother told him that when he was an infant, she once had to pull him out of a full bathtub, that he'd swallowed a lot of the soapy water and had to be resuscitated. Perhaps that explained his fears, she suggested.

So he decided not to cross Silver Lake that evening but go back to his motel. However, as he turned toward the monster Buick, something in the lake caught his eye. He looked. There was a dark object floating just beyond the circle of green light cast by the arc lamps. It was very hard to see—he wasn't sure there was anything. He moved farther out on the cement slab for a better look, but as he moved, the dark object in the lake moved too. Within seconds, it was gone.

He went back to his motel and lay on the bed in his double-breasted gray suit, trench coat and shoulder holster.

Morning.

He stood naked in front of the bathroom sink and looked in the mirror. His arm was still swollen and purple. This was probably something that should alarm him, he decided, but it didn't. He could feel no pain, and when he touched the swelling it felt hard, which he thought was good. Soft swelling was bad, hard swelling was good—he had probably read that somewhere.

He drove into Silver Lake and found it all but deserted. A man waxing his car in the hot daylight nodded cordially. Harry recognized him as the same man he'd spoken to the previous evening, the one who had come in on his sailboat.

"Fine day," the man called. "Good for all souls."

Harry nodded back. He'd put on his black fedora and he doffed it as he drove past.

Another man was apparently on his way to the lake, fishing pole and tackle box in hand, and he too nodded cordially.

Harry saw no one else, except Amelia, who was sitting on the same park bench as the previous evening.

He stopped the monster Buick in the middle of the narrow street and called, "Good morning."

She raised an arm and, without turning her head, gave him a desultory wave.

"You must like that spot," Harry added.

She nodded a little, and in the still, humid air he heard her say, "I do."

He looked at her a minute. It was clear that she didn't want to be disturbed. Why would she? She looked at peace—arms on the top of the park bench, head back. She was enjoying the warmth, the daylight and the quiet lake. What sense would there be in disturbing such contentment?

"Mind if I ask you a few questions?" he called.

She shrugged but said nothing, and her indifference wounded him.

"Am I disturbing you?"

She shook her head.

He parked the car, got out.

She called toward the lake, "Did you find what you were searching for?"

"No," he answered. "I was hoping you could help me."

She patted the bench seat and glanced back at him. "Come sit down. We'll talk."

"Okay," he said, and joined her.

She looked at him. "Harry, take off that silly hat. It went out of style a million years ago."

He nodded. "Sure." He took off the hat and set it on his lap.

"The trench coat too. You're making me sweat."

He nodded again, said, "Sorry," stood, shrugged out of the trench coat and bent over to pick up the fedora, which had fallen to the ground when he stood up.

She smiled at him as he bent over. "Harry, is that thing loaded?"

He looked at her.

She nodded at his snub-nosed .38 in its shoulder holster. He patted the gun, straightened and sat down, trench coat and fedora in his lap. "I don't know. I think so. You want me to check?"

"Does it matter?"

He shifted the trench coat and fedora to one side, pulled the .38 from its shoulder holster and held it up in front of his eyes. "Bullets," he muttered.

"So it *is* loaded?"

"Sure. Why not? What good is an unloaded gun?"

"I don't like guns, Harry. I never have. Men who carry guns are men with small cocks."

"You think so?"

"I know so."

"Would you like me to keep the gun in my car or something?"

"Lock it in your glove compartment, Harry. That will make me feel better. It will make me feel better about *you*."

He nodded. "Sure. No problem. I'll do it right now." He stood.

"Sit down, Harry. We'll talk."

He sat down.

Someone had spilled ice cream on the cement in front of the bench and a lone wasp was foraging at the edges of the puddle. Harry thought he could see a dark wasp tongue extended into the white goo.

Amelia said, "For the moment, Harry, until you become acclimatized, I'd suggest that you believe only half of what people tell you in this little community, and none of what you hear."

He smiled at her. "That's playfully cryptic," he said. "Which half of what they tell me am I supposed to believe?"

She looked at the lake again. "Would you like to go for a ride on my party boat?" she said.

The question took him by surprise. "You mean now? This moment?"

"Sure. I'll have you back within the hour. I'll give you the grand tour." She grinned. "It's really a dreamy ride, Harry. Especially when the lake's so smooth."

He shook his head reluctantly. "I can't, Amelia. Thanks anyway, but I really have to . . ."

"Look for Babs." She paused. "I'm afraid, however, that she's gone for the day. She works. I can't say where."

Barbara had a job here? The plot was thickening. "And which half of *that* am I supposed to believe?" he said.

She looked offended. "You can believe one hundred percent of what I tell you, Harry."

"Thanks," he said. "I'll keep that in mind." He stood. "Maybe you could tell me where the Alexanders live."

She stared blankly at him for a few seconds, as if trying to understand the question, then pointed at a steeply sloping street behind him. "Number fourteen," she said. "Pretty little house. White picket fence, rose trellis, cats, the whole tacky shooting match."

"Thanks," he said. "Can I take a rain check on that boat ride?"

"I'll be right here," she said.

"Good," he said, and looked expectantly at her.

"Something else, Harry?"

"Yes. A restaurant. I haven't eaten. . . ."

"What about the motel restaurant?"

"It's closed."

She shook her head. "No, it isn't. I ate there this morning. It's not closed."

"Mr. Habuda told me when I arrived that it was

closed. He said there weren't enough people staying at the motel to keep it open."

Amelia smiled. "There are now. Everyone in the community uses it. Tasty food, and homemade too."

"Thanks," he said.

He went to see if the Alexanders were home.

They weren't. He knocked on the front door a couple of times, then went through the gate of the white picket fence, under the rose trellis—and dodged a big, gaily colored garden spider in the process—to the back door. He knocked there a couple of times and looked in through a window. He saw little. An ancient refrigerator—the kind with the condenser on top, so it looks like a strange sort of alien being—an equally ancient stove and a small white enamel dining table with three bright red chairs. A huge gray Persian cat peered at him from one of these chairs.

He went around to the front again and looked in at another window.

Living room. Old, overstuffed lavender couch and chair—doilies on the arms—an upright piano. And another huge Persian cat asleep on top of the piano. As he watched, it awoke and blinked at him, as if confused. Then its mouth opened in a meow he couldn't hear through the closed window.

He saw a bare foot and calf sticking out on the floor behind the overstuffed chair.

"Good Lord," he whispered, and knocked hard on the window. "You in there. Are you all right?" He put his face to the window and cupped his hands around his eyes to shield them from the light.

The bare foot and calf were gone.

He straightened. "Damn," he whispered.

* * *

When he returned to Silver Lake a half hour later, rain had started to fall and people were everywhere. They seemed to love the rain. The day was very warm and still, so the rain itself was warm, and people were splashing about in puddles, walking hand in hand in the rain, holding their faces up to it—the same way, Harry remembered, that Amelia had tilted her face into the fading daylight.

No one had an umbrella. Everyone was dressed in street clothes that were soaked through, but no one seemed to mind. It was one of the oddest sights Harry had ever seen, and he rolled his window down a crack and called to a woman who had her arms outstretched, her head up and her eyes closed, "What's going on? Why's everyone out in the rain?"

"Come and join us, Mr. Briggs," she exclaimed. "The water is so purifying, the water is so *good*."

"How did you know my name?" he asked.

She kept her face tilted into the rain and her eyes closed, but she turned her head a bit toward him and answered, "Everyone knows you, Mr. Briggs."

Heavenly Eats

Chapter Nine

Sam Goodlow knew he was dead. He was positive of it. He thought that he had never been more positive of anything in his entire life.

Life? (Death? *Being alive* or *being dead*? Wasn't that all that the universe had to offer? No gray areas, no tenuous netherworlds, no idyllic and fragile places that grieving people could run to and find an end to their grief.)

Who really knew what life was anyway? The philosophical types said one thing, the scientific types another, and the man on the street said, "Well, I know that *rocks* aren't alive anyway." And this seemed reasonable enough, on the face of it, although no one had ever bothered to ask what rocks had to say about it.

Wasn't death *nonexistence?* No ideas, no thought, no plans, no future and no present?

Sure. It was obvious.

So, he was just as alive as anyone, although there were some who might be alive in a different *way* than he was.

It was a quandary.

He realized that he had to pee. It was a strange and wonderful sensation, a pain fraught with possibilities.

Who peed but the living, after all?

He cast about for a proper place. So many houses, so many people. He could pee in anyone's house— who would deny him a place to pee? It would be inhuman.

But the need passed as quickly as it had arrived and that made him sad.

Sad too that he found himself *plooped* down in odd places, at odd times, in front of people he didn't know.

Sometimes with awful results.

Chapter Ten

Harry went, through the rain, to the little café that Mr. Habuda owned.

It sat atop a high hill that overlooked Silver Lake, surrounded on three sides by tall maple trees. It looked as if it might once have been a railway dining car, which Harry thought was appealing, but when he tried the door he discovered it was locked.

He peered in through a window. He saw eight round tables covered by red and white checked tablecloths. Four sturdy looking wooden chairs with green upholstered seats stood around these tables. He could see no counter, no cash register and, for that matter, no kitchen. He saw a dark wood door with a rounded top and an oval window, and he guessed that the kitchen was beyond it.

The tables were bare, except for the red and white checked tablecloths. There were no catsup bottles, napkin holders, sugar servers.

Overhead, two bare bulbs hanging from simple brass fixtures lit the place dimly.

He backed away, gave the restaurant a disappointed once-over, decided yet again to forget about his hunger and went down the hill to the Alexanders' house.

They still weren't home, so he waited under the shelter of their front porch roof for the rain to stop. He thought that if they were involved, like everyone else, in the "rain dance" he'd witnessed, then they would come home when the rain let up.

He was right. The rain continued for a half hour. It formed little rivers that pushed down the sides of the narrow streets and ran off happily into the lake. And when the rain stopped, people trudged up the streets and into their houses.

June Alexander seemed pleased to see him. She smiled, saying, "I'll be right with you, Mr. Briggs," then unlocked her front door, went into the house and closed the door behind her.

He had expected to be invited inside.

She reappeared within moments, behind her front door, looked blankly at him, as if she didn't know who he was, then came out onto the porch.

"I believe," she said, "that you were looking for someone." She grinned.

He nodded. "Yes." He withdrew the snapshot from his shirt pocket and handed it to Mrs. Alexander. "I'm looking for her."

"And she is . . ." Mrs. Alexander coaxed.

Harry took the photograph back. "Her name is Barbara. I call her Babs. I was told that she lived here."

Mrs. Alexander appeared to think about this a moment, then said, "Well, yes, she did. She lived with us for some time. But she moved out a month ago."

A quick pause, then, "Mr. Briggs, your trench coat is all wet."

He shook his head. "It's all right." He glanced at himself. He was soaked. He looked at Mrs. Alexander again. "Can you tell me where she went?"

"Who can tell anybody anything, Mr. Briggs?" She smiled.

"Sorry?" he said.

"My little joke, Harry Briggs. Or should I say 'Hirsute'?"

He forced a chuckle. "Then you don't know where Babs is, Mrs. Alexander?"

"June," she said.

"Yeah, sure. June. Call me Harry."

"I thought I just did." She was smiling through this bizarre exchange. It was a cosy, self-satisfied smile—her lopsided sense of humor seemed to give her much pleasure, but Harry was becoming impatient with it.

"Listen, sister," he barked, "I ain't fooling around here. This dame is missing and I'm down here lookin' for her. You got that?"

June was all smiles. "Goodness, that's very entertaining, Mr. Briggs. Amelia told us you were a private dick, but I had no idea that you *talked* like one too."

Harry sighed. He felt as if he were caught up in a Möbius strip. "Just hear me out, would you? Barbara's husband hired me to come here and find her. So here I am, okay? He misses her very, very much." He closed his eyes briefly, then went on, "His life is . . . he asked me to tell you that his life . . ." He stopped, uncertain how to continue.

"Yes?" asked Mrs. Alexander breathlessly. "His life is what?"

"His heartache," Harry said, "is unbelievable. He blames himself for her disappearance. He . . . neglected her momentarily. It's the same old story. Treat someone badly and they . . . find better circumstances. They go off and hide. They find peace in a place that's almost completely inaccessible. It happens every day, Mrs. Alexander. Except, this time, it happened to him."

He paused. Mrs. Alexander said nothing—her round face was all smiles. He went on, "And if I don't find her, he'll . . ." He faltered, again uncertain how to continue.

"He'll what? What will he do if you don't find his wife for him? Please, tell me!"

"Listen, sister, this ain't what I came here to talk about, okay?"

Mrs. Alexander's smile faded. "How disappointing," she said.

"Now didn't you say that she lived with you for a month . . ."

"No. I said she left us a month ago. A little memory lapse, Mr. Briggs? A small problem with the synapses?"

He ignored the remark. "But she did live with you, so you probably know where she went."

"She went out of this house. I didn't inquire as to her destination and she didn't offer to tell me. We're not nosy people in this community, which is a fact you should bear in mind."

"I ain't trying to be nosy. I got a job to do."

Mrs. Alexander cut in. "Babs is going to be a mother, Mr. Briggs."

"Huh?"

"She is well into the age for procreation. Such an important age. We all have a stake in it. The little darlings we give birth to grow up and grow their own darling little breasts, and their little ovaries grow up and start spitting out little tiny eggs. It's something we all have a stake in. It's life pushing itself into the future. Life *making* the future! Because that's really all any of us have, isn't it? The future." She smiled oddly. "How can we have the past? It's gone, kaput, dead. Or the present. One moment it's here and the next moment—Pfft!—it's not. It's been replaced by something else. Some other present." She paused. "But this is the point, Mr. Briggs—we make our future from the past." She smiled again, clearly pleased with herself.

A lone wasp appeared and landed on her shoulder. Harry nodded urgently at it. "There's a wasp on your shoulder," he said. "It'll sting you. You'll get sick."

She glanced quickly at it, then at Harry. "Oh, Mr. Briggs. Don't be silly. No one gets sick here."

"They don't?"

She looked confused. "Why, Mr. Briggs, I'm surprised. Here you are, a private dick, someone who finds people, someone who has all the answers, and you obviously don't know where you are."

"Of course I do. I'm in the village of Silver Lake."

She nodded smilingly. "That's right. And Babs-slash-Barbara is staying with the Contes. They live at number twenty-six Vine Street, at the top of the hill."

Mrs. Conte opened her front door only a crack, though she smiled just as cordially at Harry as everyone else in the community had. "Babs is at work," she said. She was a matronly woman in her forties, and her face, fringed with curly dark blond hair, was round and jowly. She wore a bright green dress.

"Where does she work?" he asked.

"At a temporary employment agency, Mr. Briggs, so her workplace changes from day to day. She's like a will-o'-the-wisp sometimes. Last week, she worked at Crosman Arms. They make guns. And the week before that she worked for a car dealership on Route Sixty-four. They had her washing cars. Terrible job for a woman."

"But she does live here with you?"

Mrs. Conte nodded. "And has for some time, Mr. Briggs."

"How long?"

"Six months, I think."

"Six months?"

"Longer, really. This is July? She came to us just after Christmas. She was sort of a Christmas present. We found her under the tree." She smiled. "Just my little joke," she hurried on. "Humor is what makes us human, after all. *Hum*or, *hum*an, Mr. Briggs. They both have the same root, don't they?"

"So they do," Harry said. "Mrs. Conte, do you mind if I come in and look at Babs's room?"

"I don't mind, no. But my husband might. He's not home. He works."

"Then can you tell me what time you expect Babs to come home?"

"I would if I could, Mr. Briggs. But since I don't know where she's working this week, it would be difficult to tell you. It could be five, it could be five-thirty, it could be much later. She's a hardworking woman. Saves money. Wants to give her child the best."

"Her child?"

"Oh, yes. She's pregnant." The same odd smile he had seen on Mrs. Alexander's lips appeared on Mrs. Conte's. "Pregnant, Mr. Briggs. I'm surprised you aren't aware of it."

"Of course I'm not aware of it." He paused. "Can you tell me who the father is?"

She answered, still smiling coyly, "He's a man whose carnal works are legend, Mr. Briggs."

Harry shook his head. "You people speak in riddles, and I have to say that it's . . ."

"His name is Jim Anderson," she cut in, still smiling.

"And he lives here? In Silver Lake?"

"No."

"Where, then?"

She lifted her chin. "There," she said.

He looked. "You mean the lake?"

"I mean the other side." She turned her head a little and looked down the slope. "Do you know that there's someone watching you? I think he's been watching you ever since we started talking."

Harry turned his head round quickly and looked where she was looking. He saw a tall, fat, balding man. The man was dressed in a black suit, white shirt and wide, silver tie. He was standing a hundred yards away. He wore spats.

When Harry looked at him, the man stepped very gracefully to one side so he was hidden behind a house.

"Hey, you," Harry called. "What the hell do you think you're doing?"

"He doesn't look like one of the regular residents," Mrs. Conte said. Her voice was suddenly hoarse, as if she was frightened.

"Thanks for your help, Mrs. Conte," Harry said, without turning his head to look at her. "I'll take care of him." He patted his shoulder holster, beneath the damp trench coat, and grimaced. He'd locked his snub-nosed .38 in the glove compartment of the monster Buick. "Dammit!" he whispered.

He heard Mrs. Conte close her door.

He went down the slope cautiously, to the spot from where the fat man had been watching him, but found nothing, only the imprints of two large feet in the soft, dark, wet earth.

"I allowed them to have their own personalities, of course, and their own possessions. Each of them had first and last names too. And I made cardboard furniture for them to use in their cardboard houses. They could come and go as they pleased. They could re-arrange their furniture, they could paint, put in lawns. Whatever. They were free to do as they wished; within certain parameters, of course. They lacked for very little."

"You're talking about your dolls?"

"Of course. What else?"

"But you're talking about them as if they were actually alive."

"C'mon, Harry. Get with the program. Of course they were alive. I was a kid, remember. So my little playmates, as static as they might have been to everyone else, had to be alive to me. Jeez, Harry, weren't you ever a kid?"

"Sure. And I had imaginary playmates too."

"Oh, Harry, Harry, Harry. My dolls weren't imaginary, for Christ's sake."

Chapter Eleven

Harry didn't believe that Barbara was pregnant. He didn't believe there was a man named Jim Anderson, whose carnal works were legend. Jim Anderson, after all, was the name of the father on *Father Knows Best*, and Harry supposed that calling him, in essence, a stud was Mrs. Conte's idea of a joke.

It was 2:00 P.M. He went back to his motel room.

There was a note in a green envelope taped to his door. The note read:

> *Please don't continue looking for me. I'm all right.*
> *Everything's all right. Nothing is your fault.*
>
> B

He was back in the village of Silver Lake five minutes later. The rain had ended, the sky had cleared, the afternoon was warm and bright. And the community was deserted.

Except for Amelia, who was sitting on her park bench, arms up, head back, legs crossed. And as he approached her from behind, she lifted her arm and waved a little before he said anything. "What did I tell you, Harry?" she called toward the lake.

He sat beside her. "I feel like I'm the butt of some perverse joke," he said. "Rumor has it that Barbara is pregnant." He gave Amelia a flat smile.

She chuckled. "I don't know where these people get their sense of humor. Sometimes I think they actually have minds of their own."

He was puzzled.

She went on quickly, "The lake's so smooth today. Look at it. It's so smooth."

He looked. Something floating in the lake, a good distance out, caught his eye. He nodded. "What's that?"

Amelia said, "Do you see something?"

He nodded again. "Yes. I see something floating in the lake. Don't you see it?"

Amelia shook her head. "There's nothing floating in the lake, Harry."

"Sure there is. You're not even looking."

"Don't get excited. Of course I'm looking, and if there is something out there—something I'm not seeing—then it's probably a piece of driftwood."

He thought about this, then said, "Yes. It probably is." He sighed and looked at Amelia. "So, again, I'll take a rain check on that boat ride, okay?"

She smiled very quickly, then tilted her head back to take in the warm daylight. "I'll be right here," she said.

He turned to go, looked back and said, "How well

acquainted are you with the people in this village, Amelia?"

"Very," she answered.

"And if I described someone to you, you'd know him?"

"I would. Yes."

He shoved his hands into his pants pockets. "I saw a man. He was tall and fat, and he wore a black suit and a wide, silver tie." He stopped. In his mind's eye, he saw the man again. "Good Lord, Amelia," he went on, smiling, "this guy looked just like Sydney Greenstreet."

"Who?"

"Sydney Greenstreet. He played the villain in a lot of films from the 1940s. Don't you remember?"

Amelia grimaced. "No one like that lives in Silver Lake, Harry." Her tone was suddenly less poised, as if he had caught her off guard.

"You're certain?"

"I couldn't be more certain. For Christ's sake, Harry, *what* have you done?"

"Huh?"

"I knew you'd show up here and fuck things up. I *knew* it!"

"Amelia, I don't know what you're talking about."

"Why don't you just do us all a favor and *go away!*"

"How can I do that? I haven't found Barbara—"

"Maybe she doesn't want to be found. Maybe she's hiding from you for a *reason*."

He didn't know what to say.

Amelia nodded brusquely at the bench seat. "Sit down, Harry. We have to talk."

"We do?"

"Urgently."

He sat.

Chapter Twelve

Sam Goodlow knew that he had once lived in Boston. And that he had died there too. Run over by a madman in a Lincoln Town Car. Stowed away in the attic of a dowager's cavernous house and eaten by rats, because the dowager was a fake, because she was greedy and because she was a murderer as well. And because Sam, who had only been trying to do his job, had gotten too nosy. But the dowager had gone the way of the dinosaurs, and whatever she had been or done didn't matter anymore. And what pitifully little was left of Sam's temporal self lay quietly decomposing in a tree-dotted cemetery outside Boston.

But now Sam's memory showed him faces, buildings, skylines, swinging skirts, stray animals, a harbor bulging with boats and bilge.

It showed him rats, and he cringed.

He became queasy and light-headed, because he could hear the rats munching, chowing down, gorging themselves. He thought they sounded like people eating mouthfuls of cheesy salad.

And so he remembered picnics on lazy afternoons instead.

He remembered bee stings, sunburns and foraging ants. Kisses that found all the right places.

And what places were there now? he wondered. Femurs, perhaps, and mandibles and rictus grins.

Oh, it was good to be sure of that, come hell or high water. Good to be sure of one's final place in the great unscheme of things.

He sat.

He thumped the arms of the chair with his big hands and billowy clouds of dust rose up and wafted off. It was a satisfying thing to do, to thump the arms of an old chair and see it respond with dust.

The naked woman reappeared and stood very still in the doorway. She didn't look at him. She looked *beyond* him.

"You should see me dive!" she said.

"No," Sam said, "I don't want to see you dive." And he didn't. She made him uneasy. She frightened him. She gave him an almost unbearable pang of conscience, or guilt. Who *was* she?

And why was she following him around?

"Who are you?" he asked.

"Watch me dive," she said. Still she wasn't looking at him. Her focus was beyond him, beyond the four walls.

Whose four walls were they? Sam wondered. And what was he doing here?

He remembered something suddenly, with a sense of *déjà vu*: moving quietly through snow, trying to feel again the cool evening on his face, trying to smell just once more the heady odor of woodsmoke.

Remembered a naked woman rising from a big swimming pool that was alive with steam. Heated pool. Remembered watching as she climbed the dozen metal steps to the diving board, suspended above the blue, steamy water. Remembered watching as the water dripped from her wonderful body onto the diving board. Remembered thinking, "The water's going to freeze on that diving board. She'll slip."

Remembered . . . "Who's that?"

"Who?"

"Him, there! Hey you! What in the hell do you think you're doing?"

Remembered the naked woman flying, arms outstretched like an angel, breasts moving quickly up, as she made her stationary leaps before diving.

Mannequins Howl and Weep

Chapter Thirteen

Amelia looked at the lake. "This place is capricious, Harry. Smell that? Smell the clay? How can this place help but be capricious?"

"It's a hell of a time to be dabbling in your little fantasies, Amelia."

"It's not *me* that's dabbling, Harry." She bent over and fingered some of the dark earth in front of the park bench. She seemed incredibly adept with it. With one hand, she fashioned a perfect cube, flattened it, fashioned a ball, flattened it, fashioned the uncanny likeness of a man, flattened it, threw the dirt down. "So malleable," she said. She looked at Harry. "Just like you."

"I don't know what you're talking about."

"And so blind." She shook her head. "You can be good company, Harry. Not always. Sometimes you're simply . . . absurd. Like when you wear that getup." She nodded to indicate the trench coat and fedora, which he held on his lap. "But you're . . . someone I can talk to. I knew you were coming here, and I thought, It's okay, I can play with him."

"You can play with me?"

"You have a mind of your own, Harry, and feelings of your own, memories of your own. It's so complex. I mean—imagine this: imagine you're in a huge department store at night. No. Not at night. Forever. For eternity. And you're surrounded only by mannequins. They walk and talk and breathe. They have needs too, and desires, and memories. But these are all qualities that *you've* given them. You've dredged them up from your own life and your own creativity. So you know what these mannequins are all about. You know, more or less, how they're going to act, how they're going to respond, what they're going to *do*. So where's the challenge? Where's the spark, the difference, the *life*, for God's sake!" She paused, though not long enough to give Harry a chance to answer. "You do what you can," she continued. "But what can you really do? It's like a goddamned . . . accident simulation. Bodies everywhere dripping with blood, bones sticking out, people running around. But none of it's real, and everyone knows it. You go through the motions and emotions, but it's all a sham, it's all a *game*. It's all the wrong *kind* of game, because you're simply too much in control. It's like cheating at solitaire, or pitching a baseball game to blind hitters. For a while, it's fun. There's a perverse kind of fascination in watching things happen the way you expect them to happen, the way you've *programmed* them to happen." She looked away briefly, looked back. "Did you ever think how really bored God must be? I mean, he devises these beings he calls human and then, because he devised them, and created the

78

places they live in, the earth they live on, the stars that surround them, the little . . . spaces in the emptiness that they can flit off to when they stop breathing, he knows what they're going to do, when they're going to do it, *how* they're going to do it. Where's the fucking challenge? Where are the surprises?"

Harry said, "Amelia, you're going to have to be a little more explicit . . ."

"Then one day you find that someone else has come to play your game," she went on, ignoring his request. "A real person. Just like you. And he has his own memories and desires, and his own sort of creativity, primitive though it may be. Great! you say. Wonderful! The game grows more *real*, and more complex, more challenging. But what you didn't bargain on were his *fears*, his subconscious . . . I don't know, his predilections, his *tastes*."

A wasp appeared and settled on her arm. She took no notice of it. "But you're torn. On the one hand, you like this new element thrown into the game, and on the other, you just want to be in complete control!"

He looked at her, but said nothing. He didn't know what to say.

She went on, "I'm stuck here, Harry. I have good reason to be here. And to stay. But you don't, and I think that you should leave. For the sake of all of us."

Harry shook his head. "I can't leave this place without Barbara."

Amelia sighed. "You see only what you want to see, Harry. You're so blind. It's pathetic."

"I don't know what you're talking about," Harry said.

"Only because you choose not to. Barbara is beyond your reach." She looked at him, took off her sunglasses. "You act like you don't know where the hell you *are*."

"Of course I know where I am."

She studied him a moment, then said, "No, you don't. Suddenly it's clear. You have no *idea* where you are. Or even *what* you are. My God . . ." She put her sunglasses on again—the whole effect of taking them off and putting them on was archly theatrical. She smiled quickly, and announced, "The lake's being awfully, awfully frisky, Harry. I've never seen it like this."

"Frisky?" Harry said, thankful for the change of conversational direction.

"Wrong word," Amelia said, and sat back, arms up once more.

"Okay," Harry coaxed. "So if 'frisky' isn't the right word, what is?"

"Corrupt," Amelia answered. "That's the right word. I've decided that it's corrupt."

"Corrupt?" Harry was incredulous. "What are you talking about? Lakes aren't corrupt."

"This one is. And it's . . . inventive too. As inventive as I can imagine." She smiled coyly.

"Inventive and corrupt?" He shook his head. "This is stupid. . . ."

"Its motives are inventive and corrupt," Amelia said, still smiling. She looked as if she was enjoying some secret pleasure.

"Lakes don't have motives," Harry said.

"This one does." She paused. "Two can play at any game, Harry."

He stood suddenly and proclaimed, "I still don't know what you're talking about. If you're playing a game, then that's your business. I'm not going to play it with you."

"I'm afraid you have no choice."

"The hell I don't. I'm going to find Barbara and we'll leave this place together."

"Then you'll never leave," Amelia told him.

Chapter Fourteen

Night had come as quickly as an owl that swoops from the treetops and Harry welcomed the chance to sleep. The bed in the motel room was abnormally comfortable. The green light showing under the curtain gave the darkness a soft and cozy glow. And Harry thought, as he lay in his gray suit and trench coat—the black fedora propped on his head, so it almost shielded his eyes—that he had never felt quite so comfortable before. He was so comfortable, in fact, that he began to mistrust it. Maybe there was some kind of gas leak in the room. Maybe he was being lulled into a sleep that would last forever. But if that were true, he'd smell something suspicious, and the only smell in the room was the faint odor of flowers and newly mown grass. And as out of place as that odor was, it too coaxed him toward sleep.

He thought that he could hear the lake whispering to him. This was probably not what he was hearing, he supposed, for surely the lake was miles from the motel. But still he could hear the rhythmic *shush* of waves licking at some unknown shore, and this too added to his drowsy contentment.

Then the whisper changed. It became vaguely harsh, as if, among a hundred violins, one or two were being plucked instead of bowed. It was barely noticeable, and when he tried to concentrate on the harshness, he couldn't pinpoint it.

He propped himself up on his elbows in the bed. The black fedora fell to the floor. "Is someone there?" he whispered.

Something bumped gently into the closed door.

Was that outside or inside? he wondered. The soft green darkness told him little.

"Hello," he whispered. There was no response, so he said "Hello" aloud. The *shush* of the waves was gone now, replaced by silence.

"It's me, Harry."

The voice came and went so quickly that he didn't recognize it.

"Huh?" he said.

A hand touched him lightly in the darkness. He didn't recoil. He recognized the touch. It was Barbara's.

"Here I am, Harry."

He couldn't see her. The green darkness showed him only lumps that were chairs, an end table, a lamp.

"Barbara, I can't see you."

"Does it matter? I can see you."

"Let me see you, darling."

She appeared out of the green darkness—naked, soft, delightful. She bent over him, held herself up with her arms, lay her breasts against his neck, straddled him, then let her arms go limp, so she was lying on him.

"I've missed you," she whispered into the top of his head.

"Oh, God, and I've missed you," he said.

"Take off the PI getup, darling," she whispered.

"Yes, oh, yes."

"We'll fuck all night."

"Yes. All night."

She didn't move.

He reached down and found the waistband of his gray pants. But she was lying on him and he couldn't get to the button and fly. "Darling . . ."

She said nothing. She lay still. She seemed unaccountably heavy.

"Darling, do you think you could . . ."

"Yes?" she whispered.

"I can't seem to . . ." He strained to reach the button and fly of his pants, beneath her pelvis. "If you could just move a little."

She didn't move. She said nothing. Her body seemed to go limp.

He chuckled.

She chuckled.

"Very funny," he whispered, certain that this was a game she was playing.

She chuckled again. It was soft, low, delicious, a chuckle he loved.

He said, "Don't you want me to get naked, Barbara?"

She said nothing. Her body seemed to grow heavier.

He wished he could see her face. Her breasts were on his neck, so her neck was on his face.

"Okay, okay," he said playfully, into her neck, "so you've got me pinned. I give up."

She said nothing. She smelled of baby oil, as always. The smell was strong, almost cloying, especially because of her position on him.

"Barbara?"

"Move me," she said.

"Move you?" he said. "You don't think I can?" He chuckled. They had played this sort of game before. Often. He got his hands under her arms and pushed. Her arms moved. Her body stayed where it was. He pushed on her arms again, with the same results. He sighed. "Okay, I can't move you," he conceded. "You're stronger than I am. I give up."

"I don't."

"I wish you would."

Silence.

"Barbara?"

Silence.

"Barbara, please."

"Please what?"

He smiled, happy that she'd responded to him at least. "Could you move a little?"

"How can I do that, darling?"

He tried another chuckle, but it came out false and strained.

She said, "The mountain has come to Mohammed. Now Mohammed must move the mountain."

This was ridiculous. "Barbara, the game has gone far enough, don't you think?" He was immediately sorry for his impatience. He pushed on her arms once more. She didn't move. He chuckled falsely again. "I can't move you," he conceded. "Mohammed can't move the mountain. The mountain must move itself."

She whispered, into the top of his head, "Once a mountain has moved, it cannot move again."

He sighed. She'd never taken a game this far before. He got his hands under her hips, so his fingers were on either side of her belly, and pushed hard. It was like trying to move a tree. Good Lord, where was his strength?

"Barbara, please, I'm pleading with you. . . ."

"Don't you like my nakedness, darling?"

"Of course, but . . ."

"Enjoy it, then. Enjoy it forever."

He didn't like the sound of that. Her nakedness was wonderful, yes. But a man needed to *breathe*.

He pushed again, with the same results.

She chuckled. "Imagine that," she said, into the top of his head. "Now that you have me, I'll lie here naked, chuckling and teasing, for all eternity. Would that be too much of a good thing, darling?"

He pushed again, hoping to catch her off guard, but her body didn't move a millimeter. Where's my strength? he asked himself again.

"You know, my darling," she said, "strength comes from knowing *what* and *who* you are. You don't. I do. So, naturally, I have strength and you have none. And if I wanted to lie here forever, insinuating my nakedness upon you, I could, and would. But I don't." A moment's silence. "So good-bye."

She was gone.

And the soft green light in the room was gone too, replaced by the hazy glow of morning.

Harry blinked in confusion, pushed himself up on his elbows and looked around the room. Empty.

Something lying on the floor beside the bed caught

his eye. He looked. It was his black fedora. Flattened. Barbara had crushed it.

He picked it up, studied it. And what the hell was that all about? he asked himself.

Chapter Fifteen

A breeze pushed through the narrow streets of Silver Lake. It teased lace curtains and coaxed weather vanes into a languid spin. It played with the brackish water in birdbaths and briefly exposed the pale undersides of leaves. It whispered into the ears of a sleeping dormouse and then was itself spent and slept.

A black beetle, logy with sickness, lumbered across a dark wood floor.

Doors that were open stayed open.

Tidy beds remained tidy.

And in one neat little house, a woman lay dead. Punctured all over until she could bleed no more.

Her killer peered down and stuck the toe of his shoe into the blood that pooled around her body. Then he leaned over—a chore for him—stuck a chubby index finger into the blood and smeared a stripe across the bottom of his silver tie. "That's one," he said.

The café's big, square windows were lit brightly from within, and this pleased Harry as he climbed the high hill through early morning ground fog. He was looking forward to a hearty breakfast. Eggs, toast, sausage, pancakes. Maybe some hash browns too, and coffee, and fresh-squeezed orange juice. He was famished. After a lousy night's sleep and dreams straight out of hell, a body needed nourishment.

He could see people in the restaurant as he approached and he thought they looked happy. They wore contented smiles as they chewed. Good food created such smiles, so it was clear that the restaurant served good food.

He recognized a few of the people in the café. There was Leonard, who had bent over his car headlight, and Mrs. Conte, who had told him that Barbara was pregnant, and Mrs. Alexander, and even the old couple with whom he'd spoken upon his arrival in Silver Lake.

There were other people too, who were obviously residents. No one would come here from beyond it, as the community was too far out of the way. And the climb up the high hill was grueling. He wondered how the old couple had made it. And Mrs. Alexander.

He got to the restaurant and went in through the front door. People stopped eating and turned to look at him.

He nodded self-consciously and said, "Hello."

They continued staring.

He looked at Leonard. "Hello, Leonard," he said, and Leonard continued looking at him.

He looked at Mrs. Alexander, who had a bowl of what looked like oatmeal in front of her, and had her dripping spoon poised halfway to her mouth.

"Hello, Mrs. Alexander," he said, and she continued looking at him.

He cast about for an empty table. There were several. One was near the door which he supposed led to the kitchen, and he went to it, draped his trench coat over the back of the chair, took off his black fedora, set it on the table and sat down.

He waited for someone to come and give him a menu.

The other diners continued looking at him. He looked back, from face to face. There were no contented smiles on these faces. Eyes did not blink and mouths stayed shut. Some spoons, like Mrs. Alexander's, were poised halfway between plate and lips.

The place smelled of wet clay. The odor was very strong—it stung his eyes.

Harry said, to no one in particular, "Why are you looking at me?"

There were no answers.

"Please don't look at me."

And dutifully everyone looked away and began eating again. Contented smiles reappeared. Forks and spoons found their way to plates or between lips.

Harry heard what he supposed was the kitchen door swing open. He looked. Mr. Habuda stood behind him, menu in hand. He wore a white apron.

"Hello, Mr. Habuda," Harry said. His eyes had begun to water from the stinging smell of wet clay.

Mr. Habuda stepped forward, gave Harry a menu

and said, "Welcome to my café, Mr. Briggs."

Harry took the menu and opened it. There were only a few items listed—spaghetti and meatballs, a turkey club sandwich, mashed potatoes and liver, spinach salad. This was disappointing. Harry had hoped for breakfast. He said so, and Mr. Habuda replied, in a tone of great apology, "I'm sorry, Mr. Briggs, but we stopped serving breakfast a very long time ago."

"Really?" Harry said. "It can't be much past nine o'clock."

"I wish that it were," Mr. Habuda said cryptically, then went on, "The turkey club is very nice, and we have just gotten in two kinds of pasta—rotini and cappellini—as well as spaghetti. All of it is excellent. Our chef is still learning, but he's a quick student."

Harry nodded. "Sure," he said. "It all sounds great." But his eyes were stinging and his hunger was leaving him because of the awful, cloying smell of wet clay in the place. He glanced about, hoping to discover its source. Perhaps there was some kind of construction going on. But he saw only the diners, the tables, the sturdy wooden chairs, the clean floor.

He got up. "I'm sorry, no. Some other time." He put on his trench coat and black fedora, and went back to his motel room.

He was standing over the bathroom sink, splashing water on his face—trying to wake himself up from his lousy night's sleep—when a knock came at the door. He went and answered it.

Amelia glared at him. "Damn you!" She stormed past him, into the room. She was dressed in her white shorts and white shirt. He thought she looked marvelous.

"Damn me for what?" he asked, and shut the door.

"For *being* here!" she snapped. She shook her head. "No. Not for being here," she amended. "For *being*."

"What have I done?" He was dumbfounded.

She stared at him a few moments, then shook her head again, clearly in frustration. "It's not what you've done, Harry. I'm sorry. It's him, your . . . villain."

He sighed. "Amelia, I'm sorry, I've had a very bad night and a worse morning. You're going to have to stop speaking in riddles and tell me what's going on."

"Mrs. Pennypacker is dead."

"I'm sorry to hear that." A short pause. "Who was Mrs. Pennypacker?"

"Viola Pennypacker. A very nice woman. The nicest woman you'd ever want to know. My God, she took in stray cats. She fed the birds. She made chicken soup for sick people."

"She sounds like a marvel," Harry said, regretting the tone of sarcasm in his voice.

"It takes all kinds to make up a community like Silver Lake, Harry. Mrs. Pennypacker was an indispensable member of this community, and her loss is . . . an awful thing, just awful. The killer stuck her at least a hundred times. Do you know that? At least a hundred times. Maybe more. And she bled all over, of course. What a mess!"

"Good Lord, have you called the police?"

Amelia sighed. "I've done all that could be done, Harry, but I can only do so much. And now I have to ask you to leave Silver Lake. No, I'm *ordering* you to leave. And take that madman with you."

"What madman?"

"Your villain. Your Mr. Greenstreet. *He* did this! *He* murdered Mrs. Pennypacker."

"Listen, whoever murdered her has nothing to do with *me*."

She looked silently at him for a moment, then smiled. "Oh, Harry. You're so blind. So pathetic."

"Then perhaps you could enlighten me. What exactly am I supposed to be seeing that I'm not seeing?"

She kept silent for a moment, then shook her head. "I think that it's better, strategically, to leave you in the dark. The less you know, the less of a problem you'll be. Just hear me on this, Harry. If you decide to stay in Silver Lake, I promise that you will massively regret your decision for a very, very long time. Last night will seem like a fucking game of Scrabble."

He looked incredulously at her. "What the hell do you know about last night?" What *could* she know? he wondered.

"More than enough, Harry," she answered.

Sure, he thought, she was just talking, just picking up on what he'd said about having had a lousy night. It was no more than that. It couldn't be.

"Are you threatening me, Amelia?"

She grinned. "Yes, Harry. I am."

"And what about Barbara?"

"Forget her."

"Just like that?"

"You have no choice."

"I think that I do."

"No, you don't. Trust me."

"I'd sooner trust a sea snake."

T. M. Wright

Amelia grinned. "My point exactly." And she turned and left the room.

Harry went to the open door and watched her moving across the brightly lit parking lot. She had made him very puzzled, frustrated and angry. But he enjoyed watching her move. "Hey, sister," he called, "you got quite a walk."

She raised one arm, as she walked away from him, and flipped him the bird.

Harry smiled. What a dame.

Picnicking in the Corporeal World

Chapter Sixteen

Two picnickers in the corporeal world were swatting at bees and having a generally lousy time. They had chosen an attractive spot for their picnic and, as they were much in love, the day had looked promising. But then the bees arrived.

The picnickers had laid their red blanket out on a narrow stretch of sand on the shore of Cooper's Lake, which was really nothing more than a large pond. Most of the perimeter was swampy, so the sand looked inviting, and the picnickers wanted to be alone.

It was the red blanket that attracted the bees. And the clothes that the picnickers wore too—her multi colored flower print shirt on a stark white background and his blue T-shirt.

They were both looking for a chance to abandon the place—though neither wanted to admit that their little private love place had turned into a dismal failure—when the man pointed toward the center of Cooper's Lake and said, "Who's that?" But then he saw nothing, and he dropped his arm and looked puzzled.

"Who's what?" she asked.

"Someone in a boat. A fat man in a boat."

The day was clear and still. "I don't see anyone," she said.

"Neither do I. But he was there. Now he isn't. He was wearing a black suit, for Christ's sake. A fat man in a black suit in a little boat. It was fucking odd."

"Let's leave, okay?" she said. "It's spooky here." It was the chance she'd been looking for.

"Sure," he said. "Let's leave."

And they packed up their picnic goodies and hurried to their car.

But they weren't quick enough.

Chapter Seventeen

It was night and Harry was drifting into sleep when he heard: "Mr. Briggs? Are you awake?"

Harry's eyes popped open. He stared numbly at the dark ceiling.

The voice in the room said, "Do you know what my greatest fear is?"

"Uh," Harry managed.

"My greatest fear is that I'll have to make a living as a stand-up comedian." The man chuckled softly. The sound was very distant. "Which would be awful, because I don't know any good jokes, and if I did, I wouldn't know how to tell them."

Harry turned his head toward the room's far corner and saw the man there. He was only a dark beige, elongated lump in the darkness. "What are you doing in my room?" Harry whispered.

"Comedians," the man went on, "rely on *timing, delivery, presence*, and what do I know about such things? I know that I'd tell my joke, and then I'd laugh, which would be a cue to my audience that they should laugh too. But they wouldn't laugh, because I'm not a comedian. They'd just sit there, as quiet as the dead. *Quieter*, actually!

"It would be awful. I'd be a stinking rank amateur and I wouldn't make any money at all. The audience would boo me off the stage. Shit, I'd have to become a plumber or an accountant, and I'd spend the rest of my life trying to forget the whole thing."

Harry pushed himself up on his elbows. He thought that the man was less fearsome now. He seemed . . . lost somehow. Even pathetic. "You're not making any sense," Harry said.

"I think that I've always harbored this fear," the man said. "I don't have any other fears that I'm aware of—I'm not afraid of snakes, or of falling. And I'm not afraid of deep water either. Or death.

"It's just that I really can't remember any goddamn jokes. Good Lord, I must have heard thousands of them, *millions* of them, who knows?

"I remember *bits* of jokes, sure. Punch lines. Names of characters. I remember that lots of the jokes I heard had to do with salesmen. Farmers too. And sheep. I even remember this:

> In the garden of Eden lay Adam,
> Complacently stroking his madam,
> And loud was his mirth,
> For on all of the earth,
> There were only two balls. . . .

I know there's more, but I can't *remember*. I can't *finish* it." He paused. "Can you finish it?"

"No," Harry said. "I'm sorry. I can't."

"Sure," the man said, clearly disappointed. "Of course you can't. No one knows jokes anymore. Jokes are . . . out of date. They're passé. Like me. Like anyone."

" 'And he had 'em,' " Harry said.

"Huh?"

"That's the way the limerick ends. 'There were only two balls, and he had 'em.' I remember now."

The man laughed. "Then in that case, it's funny, isn't it? 'There were only two balls, and he had 'em.' "

The man fell silent.

"Are you there?" Harry said.

The man said, "Slowly, Mr. Briggs, we all become shadows."

And he was gone.

"Barbara, If you die before I do, I want you to haunt me."

"No. Sorry. Can't do it. I won't have the time."

"But if I went first, I'd haunt you."

"Thanks for the warning."

"You wouldn't want me to haunt you?"

"It depends on a couple of factors, I think. Most importantly, I'd have to know what you're going to look like, and smell like. Dead people tend not to be very attractive. Being dead has become socially unacceptable."

"So you're not going to haunt me if you die before I do?"

"First of all, my love, I do not intend to die before you. I intend to become a very old and very exquisite pain in the ass, and I intend to

exit this life only after great protest. And secondly, when I do die, it's not you I'm going to haunt. Hell, when I'm dead, I plan on enjoying myself."

Mr. Sloat and the Rat Puppy

Chapter Eighteen

Amelia, livid with anger, stormed into the room. Harry was holding a towel around himself: he'd been taking a shower when she pounded on the door. She gathered up his gray suit, his trench coat, his shoulder holster and underwear, which he'd piled on a chair near his bed, brought them back to him at the door and said, "Take them! Get out!"

"I'm naked," he told her.

"No, you're not. You've got a towel."

"But if I take my clothes from you, it'll fall to the floor, and *then* I'll be naked."

She pursed her lips. Even then he thought she was beautiful. "Goddammit, Harry, you were annoying in life and you're annoying even now."

"In life?"

She sighed. "Just take the damned clothes. I'll turn my head if you're modest. It's not as if I haven't seen it all before."

"You have?"

She turned her head.

He took his clothes from her. The towel fell.

She looked. She smiled. "No wonder you carry a *snub-nosed* .38!"

He scrambled to hide himself with the trench coat. "For Christ's sake, Amelia . . ."

"It was small then, and it's small now. I guess you really *don't* know where you are, and what you can do."

He wrapped himself in the trench coat. "It's not so small, sister. I've seen smaller."

She pursed her lips again. "Harry, sit down." She nodded at the bed. "We have to talk again."

He liked sitting beside her on the bed. She smelled of baby oil. As always, she was wearing her white shirt and shorts, and her good, even tan was wonderful to look at. Barbara had never been able to tan easily. She burned.

Amelia leaned forward, so her elbows were on her knees, looked sideways at him and asked, "If God wasn't God, who would he be?"

"I don't understand."

She sighed. "If God wasn't God, if God was someone else, someone imperfect, who would he be?"

Harry shrugged. He wasn't sure that he was up to a philosophical discussion. "I don't know," he said.

"I think he'd be *Mr. Sloat*," Amelia said.

"God would be Mr. Sloat?"

"It's an awful name, isn't it? It's so harsh. You don't *say* it, you *spit* it."

"Yes, I understand."

"And, whereas God—not Mr. Sloat—creates puppies and kittens and teddy bears, he also creates badg-

106

ers and maggots and rats. He creates the cuddly and the cute. And he creates the vicious, the disgusting and the awful too. Mr. Sloat, on the other hand, would get it all mixed up. Mr. Sloat would create an obscene hybrid."

"He would?"

"Of course. Because Mr. Sloat isn't God. He's imperfect. So he'd create . . . a rat puppy."

"Come again?"

"You are Mr. Sloat, Harry. So am I, actually. Because we create, but we're imperfect too. At least, though, I have some conscious idea of what I'm creating. You don't. It's your *sub*conscious at work here, and who knows what repulsive stuff goes on in a person's subconscious. We got a whiff of it with your Mr. Greenstreet, *your* rat puppy. . . ."

"Sydney Greenstreet? He's dead."

"And now there's this other person."

"What other person?"

"Red hair, tweed suit. He's running around asking questions, but who knows what *his* agenda is."

"I don't know what you're talking about, Barbara." She smiled.

He said, "Did I just call you Barbara?"

She nodded. "Yes, you did, Harry. Perhaps you're not as blind as I thought."

"I'm not blind at all. I can *see* that you're not Barbara."

She changed. Her tan lightened. Her auburn hair became blond. Her face became Barbara's face. "And now," she said, "you can see that I am."

Harry's mouth fell open.

"Close your mouth, Harry."

He closed his mouth.

*　　*　　*

"You're dead," Harry whispered.

She nodded. "And you are too."

"I am not."

"You are too."

"How?"

"You drowned. You were trying to be a hero."

"When?"

"A million years ago. Yesterday. It doesn't matter. Time doesn't matter anymore. It's great, Harry. At least it was."

"Where?"

"In the pool. *Our* pool. Remember our pool? Big, heated pool. Nice design, but with one fatal flaw, I'm afraid. The diving board was too high above the water for winter swimming."

"It was?"

She nodded. "Uh-huh. Ice. You get out of the water, you climb up to the diving board, water drips, ice forms. You leap, you slip on the ice, you hit your head, you drown. Which is what happened to me."

"I don't believe it."

"Yes, you do."

He stared at her a moment, then nodded glumly. "Yes, I do," he said. "I *remember*." It was the truth.

"This is incredible, Barbara." Short pause. "Do you want me to call you Amelia?"

"When I look like Amelia, I'm Amelia. When I look like Barbara, I'm Barbara."

"Is it going to be a little game?"

"Perhaps."

"Thanks for warning me."

"This whole thing is a game, Harry. Silver Lake. The people who live here. They're *my* rat puppies. *My* people. Remember what we were talking about, that last night, a million years ago?"

"About what comes afterward? Yes."

"Well, forgive me, Harry, but I was right. The universe *is* made of clay. At least this particular universe is. Mold it, shape it, make it into anything you want. I wanted a nice little community filled with quirky but pleasant people, and that's what I got. And then you showed up, with your own fantasies and your own agenda, and wrecked the whole thing."

"And Sydney Greenstreet is mine?"

"He's not mine."

"And this other guy too?"

"I think so. I don't see how it can be otherwise. Unless he slipped in here with you. I suppose that's regrettably possible."

Harry remembered. In his mind's eye, he saw a man with a craggy face and tousled red hair, watching from a field of new snow. "I'm afraid that it's more than possible. I'm afraid that it's true. He was watching us that night. He's the one I hollered at, remember?"

She did remember. *Hey you! What in the hell do you think you're doing?* She nodded.

Harry said, "And that guy has followed me here. I don't know why. Maybe he feels responsible for me. For us."

"Maybe."

"Because he distracted me. And you. You slipped, you fell, you hit your head—" It was a question.

She nodded. "That's what happened."

He nodded. "And I, not knowing you were in trouble, went after him, lost him, came back to the pool and there you were. Floating. On your stomach."

"I know," she whispered.

"And you were very appealing. I thought you were just . . . floating. I didn't know anything was wrong.

Not at that point. But then you floated too long. And that's when I jumped in."

"And sank like a stone."

He nodded. "And sank like a stone."

"Harry, we have a real problem, I think. It's not just—"

"Wait a minute," he cut in. "That thing I saw floating in the lake: was that *me?*"

"I think so. It's not important."

"You mean, that was my . . . subconscious creating a message for me." He was impressed.

"I think so," Amelia answered, "but, Harry, there are more important matters to discuss—"

He was on a roll. "And that body in Mrs. Conte's house? Or was it Mrs. Alexander's house—"

"That body was my doing," Amelia confessed. "It was my creation. I was having a bit of fun."

"Oh."

"Well, sure. Here you are, Mr. Macho Private Investigator. I thought I'd give you something to investigate."

"That was nice of you. Thanks."

"But it doesn't matter anymore, Harry—"

"And the spider?"

"What spider?"

"There was a spider in my car. It bit me. It made my arm swell."

"What did it look like?"

He shrugged. "I don't know. Very large. Jet-black. Long, thick legs. Red eyes."

"Death," Amelia told him.

"I don't understand."

"Come on, get with the program, Harry. It was your subconscious again. The spider represented death— black cape, red eyes. It's amazing what the subconscious can conjure up, especially when we don't know, consciously, what's going on around us. I shudder to think what you might have produced if I'd left you in the dark."

He grinned at her. "This is really fascinating stuff, Barbara—"

"Amelia."

"Amelia, yes. Sorry. I mean, think about it, think about this place we're in. Good Lord, it's a philosopher's paradise—"

"Please, let me speak."

He fell silent.

"Harry, your Mr. Greenstreet, your villain, your particular rat puppy, has gone over to the other side."

"The other side?"

"Yes, Harry." She sighed. "That's the place we came from originally. Remember? The land of the living?"

"Oh. That is serious, isn't it?"

"Fucking serious."

"What do you think he's going to do over there?"

"What you created him to do, of course. Kill people."

"I didn't create him to kill people."

She sighed again. "Oh, Harry, don't be so dense. Of course *you* didn't create him to kill people. Your subconscious did. Your subconscious doesn't give a shit what it creates. It does what it *needs* to do."

"That's awful."

"No. Just human. But it's worse than you think, Harry. I'm not sure, but I believe that since he's *your* creation, your rat puppy, the people he kills are gravitating to this little community. And tragic though it may be that they've had their lives cut short, it's even more tragic that they're coming *here*. There's not enough *room*, for Christ's sake!" She shook her head in frustration. "Two of his victims have already shown up. They're very confused, Harry. Like you, they think they're still alive, poor things. They're carrying a picnic basket around, they're looking for a sandy beach." Her brow furrowed. "Which reminds me, I'd better go let them in on the bad news, otherwise they're going to start filling Silver Lake up with *their* subconscious junk." She looked earnestly at him. "Christ, Harry, you've got to do something about this!"

"Do something? Like what?"

"Like go and find this Mr. Greenstreet, of course."

"Find him? On the other side? How do I get there?"

"How the hell do I know? If *he* got there, so can you. And take the man in the tweed suit with you."

Chapter Nineteen

Sam Goodlow thought that being eaten by rats wasn't so bad. It would be bad if it *hurt*, if he could *feel* it, if the rats' little pointed teeth sank into living skin and muscle. Then it would be bad, certainly. But, under some circumstances, it wasn't bad. It was good. It was natural. It was the way of the world. Things living sprang from things dead.

But he was so tired. Had he ever been so tired before in his life? he wondered.

Life . . . What was it? Barking dogs, meddlesome neighbors, fences, fragrances, music?

Eaten by rats? Eating rats? Pigs, cows, horses, cats? Cats? Whiskers and fleas. Never say please.

> There was a young cat from Surrey
> Whose knees were nothing but furry. . . .

Cats and nine lives and so many wives . . . Was there too little time in life for rhyme?

"Mr. Goodlow, you were saying . . ." June Alexander coaxed.

Saying? Sam wondered. Was he saying something? "Was I?" he said.

"You were. Yes." She was holding her front door open and speaking to him from behind it, as if he made her nervous.

Sam nodded. "Yes. I was . . . investigating. I feel that there is something to investigate here. That's what I do, ma'am. It's what I've always done. Investigate."

"I'm happy for you." She wasn't being sarcastic. She was smiling.

"It's a living," he said.

"And what is it you're investigating?"

His brow furrowed. "What I've always investigated, I imagine, ma'am. Errant husbands. Errant wives. Fraudulent accountants. People who aren't what they appear to be." That last made him wince. The dowager with the cavernous attic had been one of those people who weren't what they appeared to be. Thank God she had gone the way of the dinosaurs. "Dinosaurs, ma'am," he said.

"You're investigating dinosaurs?" This made Mrs. Alexander's smile grow broader.

"Possibly." Sam frowned. He fished in the pockets of his tweed suit, came up with a wallet, opened it, removed a card and held it out for Mrs. Alexander to see.

Mrs. Alexander read the card. "Then you are Sam Goodlow," she said. "And you're investigating dinosaurs?"

Sam put the card back in his wallet and the wallet back in his suit pocket. "Well," he said, confused. "I

don't think that I'm investigating dinosaurs, ma'am.
I believe that dinosaurs are extinct."

In the corporeal world, on East 79th Street, in Manhattan, in an apartment that was jointly owned by a
young lawyer named Barrow and a young advertising
executive named Freely, Harry's rat puppy was doing
what he had to do. He was on the verge of bringing
a life to a violent and vicious end.

It was Freely whose life he was planning to end,
though Freely didn't know it yet because she was
asleep, and Harry's rat puppy (whom Harry would
come to refer to as Sydney) was standing over her,
getting his bearings straight. He was all murder, lust,
malevolence. He was single-mindedly avaricious and
brilliant, which is how Harry's subconscious had designed him (because it was what any murderer worth
his salt should be). But he didn't see well in the pitch-
dark, because Harry didn't see well in the pitch-dark.
He would have flicked on a light, but he couldn't see
a light switch in the dark. So he waited for his eyes
to adjust. He had all the time in the world.

And as he waited for his eyes to adjust, Freely
dreamed. She dreamed of getting out of the rat race
of advertising and into something more fulfilling.
She'd write. Novels, short stories, poems. She'd find
an apartment in SoHo. She'd get an old Remington
Rand typewriter. She'd work long into the night, ex-
posing her soul. In her dream, she saw herself
hunched over the Remington Rand, pecking out the
words that would eventually turn the heads of civilization.

And that's when the first blow fell. The dream
Remington Rand typewriter flattened out and became

a smudge on the dream desk. Her dream self hunched forward and fought for air. But it wouldn't come. It was as if she were trying to breathe sand. Her dream self turned into a newborn robin too soon out of the egg—featherless, pink, beaky and desperate.

Then the second blow fell.

And she awoke, if only for a millisecond. She saw a huge black shape above her, silhouetted against the gray darkness in the bedroom. And she knew that the end of her life was close at hand, and she didn't want to see it.

"Death," said Sam Goodlow to June Alexander. "I'm investigating death." He grinned, happy to have found a sense of purpose again after so long.

Mrs. Alexander said, "Then come in and investigate."

And behind Sam, at the bottom of the little slope that led to Mrs. Alexander's house, Harry called, "Okay, buddy, what in the hell do you think you're doing? And don't try any funny business either. I got my gat trained on you."

His gat? Sam wondered. He turned his head, looked confusedly at Harry, who'd donned his private eye getup and had the snub-nosed .38 trained on Sam's head.

Sam said, "What's a gat?"

Harry nodded stiffly at the .38. "This, stupid! My piece. My gun."

Sam nodded. "Oh, of course. Then why don't you just call it that?"

Harry's brow furrowed. He shrugged. "I don't know. What's the difference?"

"None, I guess," Sam said. "Except that if I didn't know precisely what you had trained on me, I might have reacted in a way that would have proved painful for both of us."

Harry pursed his lips. "Just tell me what you're doing here, buddy. Now! Or my gat's gonna talk."

Sam chuckled.

"I mean it," Harry barked.

"Investigating," Sam told him.

"Yeah? What?"

"Whatever there may be to investigate. It's what I do."

June Alexander chimed in, "It's true, Mr. Briggs. I saw his card."

"You're telling me," Harry called, "that you're some kind of PI?"

Sam nodded. "Yes. That's what I'm telling you. And what are *you* supposed to be?"

"Dammit," Harry whispered. Wasn't it obvious to anyone what he was supposed to be? He called, "Just don't give me any guff, buddy. You damn well know what I'm supposed to be." He jerked the gun to indicate the slope leading to Mrs. Alexander's house. "Come down here. Now!"

"Why?"

"Why? Because I'll blow your head into yesterday's soup if you don't."

Sam grinned. This man was very entertaining. He descended the slope, stopped a couple of feet from Harry and gave him a puzzled look. "Okay, so now what?"

"Now, we talk."

"Oh, shit," Amelia whispered to herself. "Who the hell is that?" She was sitting on her park bench, on the cement slab above the lakeshore, and she was watching as a tall, dark-haired young woman, dressed

117

in what looked like blue flannel pajamas, trudged out of the lake. The woman seemed very confused. She carried an ancient black typewriter under her arm.

In the corporeal world, Henry Barrow was raining ineffectual blows on Sydney, who was hunched over Freely's body. Sydney was smoothing Freely's hair back from her smashed face, and he was mumbling lustful incoherencies at her, only dimly noting Barrow's blows.

At last, Sydney turned slightly, caught Barrow by the throat with one huge, chunky hand and squeezed. Barrow's windpipe collapsed. Two minutes later (it would have been nearer three minutes if he'd kept himself in better shape) he was dead.

Harry said, "I know you! You're the guy who was watching Barbara swim. You're a goddamned Peeping Tom."

Sam shook his head. Harry had the snub-nosed .38 pointed at his nose. "No, Mr. Briggs. I was *plooped*," he said.

"Plooped? Is that supposed to be a joke?"

"One moment, I wasn't there, in your backyard, and then I was. I was *plooped*. So how could I peep?"

"Insanity," Harry muttered. "Plooped, peeped. Does anyone around here have both oars in the water?"

"You should," he heard from behind him. It was Amelia's voice. "Because it's the only way you and your friend are going to get to the other side."

He glanced around at her. "I thought you said you didn't know how to get there."

"I lied."

"Of course."

"And besides, all I know is how to get to the . . . space in between, I guess you'd call it." She gestured at the snub-nosed .38, still pointed at Sam's head. "Put that down, Harry. I doubt that it would do you any good here anyway."

He looked at the gun, sighed and slipped it back into his shoulder holster, which was beginning to feel less uncomfortable and more like a part of his body.

Amelia continued, "Didn't you wonder why I was so anxious to take you out on my boat, Harry? Hell, I wanted to . . . tease you. Once you get out there, everything changes. It's a whole different world. Not this world or that one. Not this side or the other side. It's some . . . halfway place, I guess. I was going to take you to the edge of that place, because I think it leads all the way over."

"You *think?* You don't *know?*"

"Harry, what do any of us know? I'm as new to all this as you are."

"And what you're saying is, I've got to go out on your boat—"

"Your own boat, Harry. Sorry."

"My own boat. Why?"

"I value my boat. I don't want anything happening to it."

"I don't understand. If something *did* happen to it, you could just conjure up a new one, right?"

"Wrong. There's only one wish per customer. At least that's the way it looks to me. When poor Mrs. Pennypacker was murdered, I tried to will her back into existence. Couldn't do it. Don't ask me why. Maybe the . . . architect of all this wanted us to get it right on the first go around. Maybe He's teasing us just as we tease each other. Maybe He's as perverse as we are. Who knows? But I do know that you're not taking my boat. It stays here. You can conjure up one of your own boats, or you can use one of the rowboats, but my party boat isn't going anywhere unless I'm on it."

"So you're not coming with me?"

"Harry, this is your problem—you deal with it. I like my little village, and if it's going to be overrun by the ... flotsam and jetsam of *your* subconscious creation, your Sydney Greenstreet, I have to stay here and deal with that. Hell, I don't even *want* to go back to the other side."

Harry, standing by the shore of the lake, stared at the two-seater rowboat for a long time.

Sam, standing close by, said, "Why don't you do what she said? Conjure up one of your own."

Harry shook his head glumly. "I wouldn't know how to do that, Mr. Goodlow."

"Sam."

"Yeah, sure. Sam." He looked at him. "I'm afraid that whatever I conjured up might sink. What do I know about boats? I'm afraid of the water, for Christ's sake." He looked at the little rowboat again, then at Sam. "Do you know anything about boats?"

"I know that they float," Sam answered. "But only if they're built right."

Harry nodded. "That's my point." He noticed he was sweating. "I wonder who controls the weather around here?" he said. "It's so damned hot."

"There's another point to consider," Sam said.

"Yeah?"

Sam gestured at the rowboat. "Even if we did go out in this little boat and it sank, so what? What's the worst that could happen to us? We're dead already. So if we drown, what's the difference?"

Harry considered this for a couple of seconds, then said, "You've hit upon an interesting philosophical conundrum, my friend."

"I have?"

"Yes, and it's this: admittedly, we're dead—I accept that, you accept that, everyone accepts that—and yet, we're not *really* dead, because we walk and we talk, and we have a certain limited, if bizarre, control over our environment. Accepting that that is true, we would have to assume that we're subject to various . . . environmental and spiritual givens."

"If you have a point to make, Mr. Briggs, just make it."

"Sorry. Conditioning. My point is—can we, in every meaningful sense of the word . . . *die* here, in this place, because, in every meaningful sense of the word, we're *alive* here?"

Sam considered this. "Didn't your friend Amelia say that bullets would have no effect?"

"Ah, more unfounded assumptions. First of all, she's not my friend, she's my wife." He cocked his head. "Although that may not be strictly true anymore, considering that our marriage vows said 'till death do us part.' And secondly, you're assuming that she's right. Has she ever had a chance to try it out? Does she *know* anyone who's died here and lived to tell the tale? I doubt it."

"What about this Mrs. Pennypacker?"

"Amelia's own creation. I don't think she counts."

"So what you're saying, Mr. Briggs—"

"Harry."

"What you're saying, Harry, is that this is pretty much uncharted territory. What you're saying is that if we go out on that boat and it sinks, then that might be all she wrote for us? We will have bought the farm.

Checked into the big house. Shuffled off to Buffalo."

"Yes. That's what I'm saying."

"Shit. I thought so."

"So I guess that, philosophically and practically, the only course left open to us is to get into this little boat and see what happens." He stepped forward, put one foot over the boat's gunwale and took a deep breath. His whole body was trembling with fear.

"I'll row," Sam said.

Both Oars in the Water

Chapter Twenty

Amelia watched them go and thought how inexperienced and pathetic they looked. Harry was exquisitely overdressed for boating, and he stiff-armed the little boat's gunwales as if his life depended on it. At the same time, Sam was having a hell of a problem getting the oars in the holders. A fitful breeze had come up—Amelia too wondered who controlled the weather here—and the boat was pitching and yawing unpredictably. At one point, Harry had to duck to avoid being slapped across the face with an oar. It would have been comical under other circumstances, but Amelia found herself unaccountably concerned. She hadn't wanted Harry to show up but had known he would. And now that he was here, her feelings were mixed. Sure, he could be aggravating. He could be dense. He could even be a stiffneck at times. But he had a certain nerdy charm, he was agreeable to play with and she had more than once wondered if she might actually *love* him.

She was watching from the park bench where she often sat and the little boat was not far off. She thought she could even call to Sam and Harry and wish them good luck. But no. The wind was too strong, they'd never hear her.

Rationalization, she realized. The wind wasn't too strong. She simply didn't want Harry to know that she was concerned.

"Maybe this wasn't such a good idea," Harry called to Sam, who had finally gotten the oars engaged in the holders and was doing his best to get the boat moving against the wind. "I mean, I think there's a storm coming."

Sam looked at the sky. His brow furrowed. "Did you notice that there's no sun here?" he said.

But Harry hadn't heard him above the wind. "What?" he called.

Sam repeated himself. Harry looked up and saw only a bright blue, cloudless sky faintly tinged with green. "Do you think," he called, "that there are actual weather patterns in this place?"

Sam shrugged.

"And even more interesting," Harry continued, "do you think there are actual *directions*—north, east, south, west."

"Sure," Sam answered. "Why not? People made up that stuff in the first place, so they could know where they were, I guess. And so they could know how to get where they wanted to be. We're people. We can make up our own stuff."

Harry—despite the fact that he hadn't been out on a boat in decades and was as nervous as a cat—managed a quick smile. This guy was brighter than he'd thought. "So," Harry said, "if we want to say that back that way"—he pointed toward shore—"is west, then that's what it is."

Sam nodded. "Which would mean that that way"—he pointed left—"would be north and that way"—he pointed right—"would be south and straight ahead would be east."

Harry, whose back was to the shore, looked beyond Sam, at the opposite shore, which seemed to be no more than a mile away. "We just head east," he said.

"Huh?" Sam said. The wind was building.

They were fifty feet out now and the water, which had been a brownish blue nearer to shore, was becoming a deeper blue, closer to the color of the sky, as they moved farther from the shore. This made Harry uncomfortable, though he wasn't sure why. "East," he called. "We go east."

Sam nodded, and kept rowing.

In the corporeal world, on Fifth Avenue, in Manhattan, Sydney had pulled out a wad of bills and was attempting to pay for a room at the Ritz Carlton with it. But the dapper man behind the counter was looking at the bills as if they were disease-laden, because they were grotesque fakes. They looked as if a child had drawn them with smudgy green crayon (which was the way that Harry's subconscious had seen the money that Sydney would carry—ill-defined, a necessary inconvenience. What real use, Harry's subconscious reasoned, did arch villains have for money?).

The desk clerk at the Ritz Carlton couldn't decide whom to call first—the police or hotel security. But he knew instinctively that he shouldn't make Sydney angry. "Sir, if you could just wait a moment, I'll check on room availability."

Sydney spoke. His voice was a raspy, nasal tenor that was irritating and threatening at the same time. "My good man," he said, "you've already checked on room availability. I think you're giving me the runaround, and I don't like it. Either my money is good here or it isn't."

It was then that the desk clerk noticed Sydney's wide silver tie. Near the bottom, it bore several diagonal red stains. The man centered on these stains and whispered, "Good Lord, is that blood?"

Sydney looked at the stains, took hold of the tie, lifted it to his nose and sniffed. Then he put the tie neatly back in place and gave the desk clerk a sinister, meaty smile. "Strawberries," he said.

The desk clerk stared wide-eyed, but could say nothing.

Sydney nodded at the wad of grotesquely fake bills that the desk clerk clutched in his hands. "I'll take that back now," he said. "Your hotel is not to my liking." The clerk quickly handed the bills over and Sydney left the hotel. His stride was quick, fluid, elegant. Watching him, the clerk couldn't imagine how someone so large could move like that.

Harry offered to row, but Sam was enjoying himself.

"I remember, when I was a kid, my parents would take me up to a cabin they owned in the Adirondacks. It was on a lake—hell, pretty much like this one. And I used to take our rowboat out all the time because it was so peaceful on that lake. Especially in the mornings, when there was a fog. It was like I was in another world."

Harry nodded. The wind had calmed. Conversation

was easier. "And now you *are* in another world."

"Am I?" Sam said.

Harry couldn't decide if Sam was simply being ironic or if his question had been genuine.

Sam went on, "How can we know for sure exactly *where* we are? I mean, I guess we know where we've come from, in a way. But where was *that*, for God's sake?"

"I think we have to make a few logical assumptions, based on empirical evidence," Harry began, but Sam cut in.

"I'm *here*, now, in this place, and I was *there*, in that other place—the earth, the real world, whatever you want to call it. And when I *was* there, I thought I knew where I was and what *it* was. I assumed all kinds of things. Everyone does. It's like this, Harry: what if I'd lived, all my life, in a single room? Like a mouse in a box. That would have been my universe, and I would have guessed that that was the extent of the universe. But then one day a door opens and I'm allowed into *another* box, another room. What do I assume then? Do I assume that the universe consists of just these two rooms? Hell, no. I assume that if there are two rooms, there must be three, or four, or four hundred, or four hundred thousand. Unless I'm a white mouse. Then I assume that there are just two rooms. But I'm not a white mouse." He grinned, pleased with himself. His grin was broad, toothy, full of good feeling.

The wind picked up again. Harry grabbed the gunwales. "Shit," he whispered.

But Sam was caught up in his monologue. He even forgot to row. The oars sat useless in the churning water. "But maybe we can't even assume anything about white mice. We think they're not as bright as

129

we are because they don't build cars and make war. But does that make them stupid? No. It makes them smart, because they don't endanger their own existence. White mice will outlive us all, Harry."

The water was sloshing over the gunwales now. It was the same color as the sky and this made Harry very nervous. He remembered what the man in the olive-colored Speedos had said: "It's frighteningly easy to become disoriented. Sky, land and water seem to merge, and eventually you begin to feel that you're simply . . . floating. It's very disconcerting, Mr. Briggs. You can't imagine." But now Harry *could* imagine, and only too well. Because when he looked beyond the grinning Sam Goodlow, who was still yammering about white mice, he couldn't see the opposite shore. He saw only the deep blue-green sky, the deep blue-green water and just the barest hint of a horizon.

He turned his head and stared back toward Silver Lake. He saw a whisper of brown and green, as if he were looking through fog. But there was no fog. "Row, Sam!" he shouted.

Sam didn't respond. He was still talking, although Harry couldn't hear him above the noise of the wind and water.

"We've got to go back!" Harry shouted.

Sam stopped talking at once. "Back?"

Harry turned halfway around and pointed toward the near shore. It was all but gone now. "Row, dammit! We've got to go back!" He grabbed the gunwale again. The boat was threatening to capsize.

"No shore!" Sam called.

Harry turned around in the seat and looked toward Silver Lake again. He saw a churning, deep blue-green sky and churning, deep blue-green water.

"Where do we go?" Sam shouted.

A wave as tall as a man swept over the boat and soaked them both to the skin. The water was icy cold. *Dammit*, Harry thought, and shivered. He was dead already, and now he was going to die again of hypothermia. Unless he drowned first, which seemed more likely.

"Exhilarating!" Sam called, and Harry had to look up at him because the boat was riding the crest of a huge wave, the oars were touching nothing but air and Sam—tweed suit, tousled red hair, craggy, smiling face—was at an oblique angle *above* him.

"I didn't hear you!" Harry called.

"What?" Sam called back. He was still smiling. He was having a hell of a time.

"Row, Sam!" Harry called. He thought he was going to pee his pants.

Amelia quickly lost sight of them. The wind picked up and the little boat seemed to merge with the sky and water. And now it was gone.

She sighed. So, there was loss in this life too. It hardly seemed fair.

In the corporeal world, on East 42nd Street, in Manhattan, it was early evening, and Sydney had slit the throat of a young Wall Street executive named Morgan Brown. It had taken several minutes for the man to die of suffocation, and Sydney had enjoyed every moment. "Thank you, that was pleasant," he whispered, when Brown's gurgles and pleas were done and he was quiet.

Then Sydney bent over, dipped his chubby index finger deep into Morgan Brown's wound, wiped the blood diagonally across his wide, silver tie, reached into the pocket of Brown's suit jacket and got the man's wallet. Brown had been looking forward to a vacation and was carrying lots of money. Sydney straightened and counted the notes with delight.

Harry's subconscious had been wrong. Sydney needed money. He couldn't *kill* his way into fine hotels. The Brown Derby wouldn't serve him steak tartare if he disemboweled the chef. Murder was wonderful, certainly. Nothing else piqued his libido in quite the same way. But money opened doors and made people grovel.

They'd been fighting the wind and waves for what seemed like hours. Each new wave had threatened to send them both plunging into nothingness. Even Sam's *Gee, this is fun!* grin had faded, and he had frantically tossed himself around in the boat in an effort to keep it balanced in the water. Meanwhile, Harry, his head down and his eyes closed, accepted that this was going to be his punishment for a life of nonproductivity and uncertainty: he was going to spend eternity in this little boat, with this crazy man, convinced that the next wave would bring an end to his existence. Whoever God was, he certainly had a sense of humor!

Then, in an instant, the wind and water calmed. Harry opened his eyes and whispered, "I don't believe it." He could see land.

"That's New York City," he said.

Sam nodded wordlessly.

"My God, there's the Statue of Liberty, the World Trade Center, the UN."

Sam nodded again.

"How the hell did we get here?"

Sam shrugged, but said nothing. He looked glum.

They were a couple of miles offshore, Harry guessed, and the ocean was as still as ice.

He said, noting Sam's glum look, "What's wrong with you?"

Sam answered, "See that?" and nodded.

Harry turned his head, looked. He saw something large, dark and roughly circular floating not far off. "Uh-huh," he said. "What is it? It looks like garbage." He turned to Sam again.

Sam shook his head. "It's not garbage-garbage. It's sewage. It's shit."

Harry looked again. The circular darkness was as large as a football field. "That's a lot of shit," he said.

"It's a hell of a lot of shit."

"Where did it come from?"

"There?" Sam nodded toward shore. "From them. From us."

"I see."

"No, you don't."

"But I do. I see. *They* shit and here it is. What could be simpler? What else is there to see?"

"Nothing. The question is, what do you *smell?*"

Harry sniffed the air. He frowned, sniffed again.

Sam said, "You don't smell anything, right?"

Harry sniffed a third time. "I don't know." A fourth time. Another frown. "You're right. I don't smell anything."

"That's what's wrong. Either our noses have stopped working, or this is not the place it appears to be, or it *is* the place it appears to be and we're not really here."

Harry nodded. "The possibilities are endless."

"I hope not," Sam said, and brought the oars up out of the water to rest them on the gunwales. "And there's another thing: where's the sun?"

Harry cast about in the sky above. It was deep blue, cloudless. "Oh, hell," he whispered.

"Again, I hope not," Sam said, and added, "Take off your hat."

"Take off my hat? Why?"

"Just take it off."

Harry reached, grabbed the brim of the black fedora, pulled. The hat stayed put. "Good Lord," he whispered, and pulled harder. The hat wouldn't come off. It was as if it were a part of his head.

"And how about the coat?" Sam said.

Harry tried to take off his brown trench coat. He couldn't.

Sam sighed. "I thought so," he said. "All that wind—"

"You thought what?" Harry said.

"We're partway there. This is a kind of ... place in between. Isn't that what Amelia called it? All the physical trappings are here, but it's like a ... snapshot, I guess. At least to us."

"Or a frozen computer program."

"Sorry?"

"You know, you're in the middle of a computer game, or Lotus, or whatever, and suddenly the thing freezes up. You punch all the keys, but nothing happens."

"Oh, yeah, I understand," Sam said, though he obviously didn't.

"And what you have to do is reset the thing."

"You mean, press a button and get it to start over again?"

"Uh-huh."

"It would be nice if it were that simple."

"You're saying it isn't?"

"I don't think it is. But what do I know? I've done

a bit more . . . traveling than you have, it's true, but I'm not sure of anything. I'm just guessing."

"And your guess as to why I can't take off my hat and coat?"

Sam shrugged. "Because they're a part of you?" It was a question.

Harry thought about this. "I think I understand. There is no real *me* anymore. No physicalness. No body. Only spirit. I see my hands and my feet because I expect to see them. And I see the trench coat and hat because I expect to see them too. Because I've made them a part of me. I might as well try to take off my head."

"Maybe," Sam said.

"But back there, in Silver Lake, I *could* take my clothes off, and I did."

Sam grinned ruefully. "If I had all the answers, I'd still be alive," he said.

"Yeah," Harry said. "Me too."

"Dammit to hell," Amelia whispered as the well-dressed young man trudged up from the lake. He saw her, smiled, waved and called, "Hi there. Is this Club Med?"

Chapter Twenty-one

In the corporeal world, at Manhattan's 10th Precinct, Detective Kennedy Whelan was dog tired. He wondered if he had ever been so tired before. Sleep wouldn't cure it, he knew. Even if he slept for a week, he'd wake up tired.

He dabbed at a coffee stain on his shirt and grumbled a curse. When he grew tired he became clumsy, and when he became clumsy, he got surly. It was time to go home. He crumbled his big cigar out in an ashtray.

His partner came over, put a thin file folder on his desk and said, "Here's another one." He paused. "You look like last week's vegetables, Ken. Have some coffee. Get laid."

"In that order?" Whelan asked, and flipped open the file folder. He saw an eight-by-ten color photo first. It showed a nattily dressed man in his midtwenties, lying on his back, his hands clutching the air near his throat. Blood had pooled around him like a shawl. His eyes were open very wide and one leg was sharply bent.

Whelan's partner said, "Samuels and Tower had this one, Ken, but Tower's wife got sick, so now we have it. Their report is in the file."

"Motive?" Whelan asked.

"The guy's wallet was empty."

"It was robbery, then?"

"I think so. It's hard to say whether he got his throat slashed as an afterthought or not. It probably doesn't matter."

"No doubt you're right," Whelan said, and closed the file. "I'm going home, Mike. Jesus, I feel like a third-year medical student. I've been up for days."

"Sure," his partner said, as Whelan stood. "Everything will be right where you left it when you get back."

"Yeah, thanks a lot," Whelan said drily, then took another cigar from his pocket and lit up.

"See it?" the man on the yacht said, and pointed stiffly toward the horizon. "See it, Doris?"

Doris, who was nearsighted, looked but saw nothing, and said so.

The man said, "A little boat. What's it doing way out here?"

"What I want to know," Doris demanded, "is what *we're* doing way out here! It's winter, Charles."

"Mine was a rhetorical question, Doris. *Rhetorical.* That means I wasn't really asking what it was doing out here, and even if I was, why would I ask *you?*"

"That's very unkind, Charles. Why are you so unkind?"

Charles ignored her. "There's no one in it," he said. "The boat's empty."

"Empty?" said Doris.

The boat vanished.

Charles, who had been sitting in a deck chair, jumped to his feet and ran to the stern rail. "Doris, it's not there. The boat's not there anymore!"

Doris strained to see. "Did it sink?" she asked.

"Well, it must have."

"We'd better get over there, then. Maybe someone's in trouble."

"For God's sake, Doris, don't you think I know that?" Charles snapped, and went to start the yacht's big engines.

Harry said, "Listen. Do you hear that?"

Sam listened. "Yeah. A motor."

"Boat motor, I think. Or an airplane." He looked about, saw the Manhattan skyline, a quiet blue sky, still blue water. But he saw what looked like snow too, and this confused him. Snow and blue sky at the same time? Someone was mixed up. Someone didn't know what *date* it was.

"No," Sam said. "It's a boat." He listened for a few seconds. The engine noise grew louder. "Whatever it is," he said, "it's coming this way."

Harry cast about frantically for some sign of the boat. It was very disconcerting to see the Manhattan skyline with such clarity, the blue sky, the blue water, the floating sewage and the snowfall overlying all of it, but not the boat that was clearly very close, and drawing closer with each second. "I don't like this," he whispered. "Damn, I don't like this."

"You and me both," Sam said.

"I mean," Harry said, "maybe it's like matter/an-

138

timatter or something. Maybe if they come in contact with us, we'll all explode. Or implode. Or just . . . stop existing."

"And would that be so bad?" Sam asked.

"For me, it would be," Harry said at once.

Sam nodded. "For me too."

Charles throttled the engines back and brought the yacht to a slow stop. "Doris, do you see anything?" he called.

Doris, standing at the stern rail, leaned over and looked left, right. "It must have sunk, Charles."

"I *know* it sank, for pity's sake. But do you see anyone floating there? Do you see any bodies?"

"Bodies? Charles, I didn't know that I was looking for *bodies*."

"Well, you aren't looking for pennies from heaven, Doris."

"You're an unkind man, Charles—"

"Wait a minute. There it is!" Charles called. Doris looked at him. He was pointing toward the horizon. She looked, but saw only a faint gray smudge.

"That can't be it, Charles!" she proclaimed. "It's too far away."

"But it is, Doris. It is!"

"Oh, Charles, you're so full of crap. I think you're going to explode some day, you're so full of crap. Bringing us out here in the winter just because you miss your boat. You're so full of crap."

Charles's mouth fell open. "Doris, you can't speak to me like that!"

"Where did it go?" Harry asked.

"You mean Manhattan?" Sam asked.

"Yeah. It's gone. It's not there anymore." They

were surrounded by ocean and sky. The ocean was becoming frisky. Whitecaps were forming and the sky was smudging over with ominous, frothy gray clouds.

"We're in deep doo-doo!" Sam said.

"Up to our belly buttons," Harry said.

Freely didn't believe what Amelia was telling her, but she was too well mannered to admit it. She said, "In other words, what you're saying is . . ." She cocked her head, smiled pleasantly. "Are you married?"

The abrupt change in the conversation took Amelia by surprise. "Yes. At least, I *was* married."

"Divorced, then?"

"No. Not divorced. Not single. Not married. *Dead*. Like you. That's what I've been trying to say, Miss Freely."

"Oh, I know what you've been saying, Amelia." She was a delicate-looking woman, with clear, creamy skin, a small nose and large, expressive green eyes. "And believe me, I'm not disputing it. If you tell me I'm dead, then that is what I am, and it's what I believe."

"You think I'm nuts."

"I think, Amelia, that this is a very pleasant little community you have here, and if a person *were* to die and go off to another world, then this would be precisely the world she would want to go off to."

Amelia sighed. "Miss Freely—"

"Anna."

"Of course. Anna, I'm going to show you something very strange. Something you have never seen before. Something that may shock you."

"I'm not easily shocked, Amelia. I've seen it all."

"No. You haven't seen this." She turned her head. When she turned back, she had become Barbara.

Freely smiled. "Yes?"

"Yes what?"

"I'm waiting."

"Waiting for what?"

"For you to show me whatever it is you are intent on showing me."

"But I am. Here it is. I'm someone else."

"Are you?"

"For Christ's sake, can't you see? I'm a different person."

"In what way?"

"In every way. Different eyes, different hair, different skin, different body."

Freely stared at her for a moment, then asked, "Is there someplace I can stay, while I'm waiting to go back?" She smiled. "I have American Express."

"Blue sky," Harry said.

"And a calm sea," Sam said.

"Too calm."

Sam nodded. "I can see us playing this maddening little game for a very long time. Christ, we should have stayed where we were."

"Perhaps, but we didn't. And there were problems we were asked to solve, remember?"

"We?"

"You're getting testy," Harry said.

"I am and I'm sorry." He didn't sound very sorry. He looked about. "Damn, not even a bird. Where are the birds? There should be birds. But there's nothing. It's all so . . . dead!" He grinned, pleased with his irony. He looked at the ocean. "But who knows *what's* down there!"

"I wouldn't want to find out."

"We may have no choice," Sam said.

"You may be right."

Sam looked at the water for another minute, then turned to Harry. "How deep do you think it is?"

"Deep? It's the ocean. It's a couple of miles deep."

"Is it? It looks like the ocean, sure. But, then again, *you* look like something out of Mickey Spillane."

"Thanks."

"You're missing my point."

"No, I'm not. I get your point. Maybe we're not seeing what's really there."

"Uh-huh." He reached over the gunwale and fingered the water. "Know what it feels like?"

"Ice water."

"Nope. It feels like air."

Harry reached tentatively into the water, then looked at his fingers. "You're right. There's nothing to it."

"Or nothing to us."

"You're going around in circles. First, there's nothing to the water and now there's nothing to us. It can't be both ways."

Sam thought about this, then nodded. "You're right. It's got to be one way or the other."

"And we *know* that there's something to us, because we're discussing it."

"It?"

"Yes. We're discussing whether there's something to us or not. If there was nothing to us, then we wouldn't be discussing it."

Sam thought about this, then said, "That sounds like a lot of bullshit."

Harry frowned. "It does, doesn't it."

Sydney's accent was imperfect. A rat-puppy invention, it was a rattling combination of Middle Eastern,

142

English and Bostonian that clattered and rolled off his tongue like marbles on sandpaper. But it was so imperfect that it fooled almost everyone into believing that it was a real accent they'd simply never heard before.

Like the man at the shoe-shine stand at Grand Central Station, who gave the toes of Sydney's black shoes—peeking out from beneath his spats—a blazing shine. "Where you from?" the shoe-shine man asked. "That accent's a new one on me."

"Casablanca," Sydney answered, with some uncertainty. Up to that point, he had had no reason to think about where he was from.

"Is that in New York State?" asked the shoe-shine man.

"I don't believe so," Sydney answered, for, in truth, he wasn't sure where Casablanca was, because Harry wasn't sure where it was. "I believe that it's somewhere in Africa," he went on.

"Yeah," said the shoe-shine man, and when Sydney got up, he added, "Merry Christmas."

And there was the man at a Hot Sam kiosk not far from Grand Central who said, "Canadian, huh?" as he handed Sydney a fresh, steaming pretzel. Sydney looked quizzically at the pretzel for a moment, then bit into it. His villainous, chubby face brightened and he chewed hungrily.

"Alberta?" the man pressed on.

"I'm from Casablanca," Sydney told him.

"You mean like in the movie?"

"Exactly," Sydney said, and took another hungry bite of the pretzel.

"You know you look just like Sydney Greenstreet," the man said.

"That's very possibly because I *am* Sydney Green-

143

street," Sydney proclaimed as he chewed.

The man grinned and nodded. "You want another one of those?"

"Oh, yes. Two more. No, three!"

Again, Sam and Harry were sitting in their little boat on a dead calm, blue-green ocean, under an empty blue-green sky. The oars rested on the gunwales. Harry sat with his elbows on his thighs, his hands clasped in front of his knees and his head down a little. He had tried to adjust the black fedora so it rested farther back on his head, but it was stuck in place.

Sam was leaning backward, with his elbows on either side of the bow. His fingers were laced over his stomach. He said, "I'd give anything just to have a seagull fly over. A real seagull."

Harry nodded glumly. "We were so stupid to believe we could go back. What were we thinking?"

"Hell," Sam said, "I wouldn't even mind if the damned thing *shit* on me."

"We're *ghosts*, Sam! Spooks! The undead! What right do we have to insinuate ourselves on the living? I mean, remember all those ghost stories we heard on the other side, Sam? Invariably, the ghost was in one way or another not all there. Either he was physical but invisible, or visible but fuzzy, or translucent, or transparent, or physical and visible but voiceless and temporary. That should have told us something. I know what it tells me now. It tells me that you and I are trying to go someplace we *can't* go. It tells me that we're trying to be something we can't be. Like slugs trying to attend the opera." He looked at Sam. "Am I making any sense?"

"Sense?" Sam asked, because he hadn't been listening.

Harry lowered his head again. "Of course not. What sense can the dead make?"

"How did *he* get over?" Sam asked.

"He? You mean Sydney?"

Sam nodded. "Yeah. How did he do that?"

It was a very good question, Harry thought. Up to that point, they had supposed that they were simply going to follow Sydney over, as if he had blazed the trail and they were going to take it. Obviously, that wasn't happening. But Harry didn't have an answer. "I don't know," he said. "Do you?"

Sam shook his head. "I haven't a clue."

"Uh-huh. Well, *you're* supposed to be the real private investigator here."

"I investigated cheating husbands, and missing wives and people who were trying to cook their company's books, Harry. Your Sydney Greenstreet doesn't fall into any of those categories." Sam was upset.

"Sorry," Harry said. "I just thought you might know how we should approach the problem."

"No, I don't."

"I thought you might know what questions to ask. Isn't that where any real investigation begins? By asking the right questions?"

Sam nodded. "And it ends by coming up with the right answers. We can ask all the questions we want, Harry. Hell, we've already started. But if we don't have a prayer of coming up with the right answer, it doesn't matter. The simple fact of asking a lot of brilliant questions isn't necessarily going to provide us with brilliant answers."

"I see what you mean."

"Though, of course, we might ask ourselves what's different about Sydney." He cocked his head and grimaced. "But that's stupid. If he has or does something that we don't have or do, then it's like asking why birds fly. They fly because they have hollow bones and feathers. We *can't* fly because we have solid bones and no feathers, and we also have no hope of *changing* that fact."

"Sydney has time," Harry said.

"Time?"

Harry nodded. "He has time. Like . . . clocks ticking. You said it yourself, Sam."

"Don't we have time too?"

"I don't think so. We have eternity. But I don't think we have time."

Sam smiled. "You're flinging bullshit again."

Harry shook his head. "No. I think I'm on to something. Think about it, Sam. Look around you and think about it. What is this place we're in? What words describe it? Featureless. Changeless. *Time*less."

"Harry, your Sydney Greenstreet *isn't human*. He doesn't have time. He doesn't have anything."

"Sure he's human. I made him human. My subconscious gave him all the important . . . facets of a particular human being. Tall. Overweight. Balding. A grim and ironic sense of humor. Fifty years old." He leaned forward and looked Sam in the eye to emphasize what he was going to say next. "And in a year, Sam, he'll be fifty-one. Last year, he was forty-nine. This is the way he sees himself because it's the way I created him. Myself—I'm forty-eight. Last year, I was forty-seven. Next year, I'll still be forty-eight. And the year after that, and the year after that too. Hell, in ten thousand years, I'll still be forty-eight, because I'm stuck in eternity. Just like you are. But not Sydney. I gave him an age. I gave him *time*. That other world, the world of the living, is in the midst of time. That's why people go to college, and get married, and write books. Because they have *only so much* time. But not us. Not you and me. We have forever. So we don't have time in the same way that the *living* have time. Do you understand?"

"I don't know. I still say it sounds like bullshit." He looked very confused.

Harry sighed. How could he explain what he was talking about? He pointed at the calm ocean. "Think about it this way, Sam. Say you find yourself, all at once, in the middle of the ocean. I mean, surrounded by water. Say you're drowning and you're in the middle of the water. You need desperately to breathe. And you know one of two things. You know either that you are surrounded by water and that it stretches to infinity above you and below you. Or you know that you are only a couple of dozen feet from the surface. If you know the former, then you do nothing. You resign yourself to drowning. What can you do? There is no place to go. But if you know the latter, that the surface is only a couple of dozen feet above you, you try like hell to reach it." He smiled, pleased with his analogy. "We know, deep down inside us, that we don't have *time* because we are surrounded by eternity. Try measuring eternity. Try breaking it up into little bits—eons, centuries, years, days, hours, minutes, seconds. You can't, because eternity itself is unmeasurable. So, time, as the living usually think of it, has no meaning for us and consequently our attempts to do something *inside* of time—like cross to the other side and find Sydney—are useless."

"I think," Sam began, still stuck on what Harry had said about the drowning man, "that either way you

147

try like hell to reach the surface. No matter how far up it is. It's called the will to *survive*." He smiled too, certain that he'd blown Harry's argument away.

Harry shook his head. "That's the point, Sam. How can we *survive* anything? We're already dead."

"But you said we weren't. You said that *here* we're alive."

"And where is *here?* It's an endless loop. It's the stuck computer program. Don't you see? Our . . . real selves know that we're stuck in eternity. Our real selves *know* that we're immortal. So we simply cannot do what mortals do."

"Unless we can convince our inner selves that we're not immortal."

"It sounds good to me."

"Me too."

"So how in the hell do we do that?"

Prisoners of Time

Chapter Twenty-two

Kennedy Whelan, driving his Ford Crown Victoria to work at Manhattan's 10th Precinct, crossed the George Washington Bridge just as a Coast Guard cruiser was beginning to pass beneath him, on the Harlem River. It was responding to a report that a small rowboat was apparently adrift, and empty, several miles out in the Atlantic. Whelan took no notice of the cruiser. He was intent on other things—on the eight-by-ten color photo of the young man whose throat had been cut. On the coffee and Danish waiting for him at the little bakery next door to the precinct house. On the possibility that he might get back to the apartment after his shift ended in time to watch the Rangers play the Sabers.

He glanced at his watch. Christ. He'd been up for nearly three days, but he'd slept for less than six hours, because his damned internal alarm clock had awakened him at 5:30 in the morning, just as it had every morning for the past twenty years. And, once he was awake, it was impossible for him to get back to sleep.

He turned on the radio. Morning drive-time drivel. People talking about getting laid in strange places—in closets, in the trunks of cars, on an ironing board. He changed channels, got an oldies station, listened for a minute to "Peggy Sue," changed channels again, got a sports report and turned the dial back to the drivel.

On Houston Street, in Greenwich Village, a man in his early twenties was robbing a store owner who was in his late sixties. The young man, whose name was Patrick, had a sawn-off shotgun pointed at the store owner's forehead and he was giving him an ultimatum: "You open that safe in ten seconds or I'm going to blow your brains all the way into the middle of next week." And he started counting. Slowly. "One . . . two . . . three—"

The store owner, whose name was George, thought a couple of things as he stared into the wide barrel of the shotgun and listened to the young man count. He thought that "blow your brains all the way into the middle of next week" was an interesting turn of phrase for a hoodlum to conjure up. He thought, also, that the young man was probably going to kill him, regardless of whether he opened the safe or not. And he thought that if that happened, it wouldn't be so tragic, because his life had been basically satisfying and having his brains blown out was probably one of the quickest and most painless ways to die. He thought too that he should be more frightened. It was true that his knees were quivering and his stomach was fluttering, but the idea of dying didn't bother him as much as he supposed it should. He wasn't sure why. He guessed it was because it was all so *inevitable*. If this young hoodlum didn't kill him now, then he would die soon enough in some other way. In a couple of months, another young hoodlum might come along. Or, in five years, he'd develop some terminal illness, as several of his friends had. Or, in fifteen, or twenty, or twenty-five years, he'd go to sleep and simply not wake up. Did it really matter *when* it happened?

These were certainly heady thoughts for a man whose life was hanging on a crazy person's count to ten, George knew, and this knowledge gave him a little blush of pride. And so he smiled, despite the shotgun staring him in the face.

Then, because Patrick had grown tired of waiting for George to open the safe, and because he had long since finished counting to ten, and because he was sick to death of people not giving him any respect—which was why, he was convinced, George was smiling—he blew George's brains out. Then he stared for a long moment in deep fascination and disbelief at what he'd done, threw the shotgun to the floor and bolted out of the store in a panic.

A UPS truck, driven incautiously by a man named Arthur, slid on a patch of ice and ran him down a couple of minutes later. Patrick died almost immediately.

And as he stood and stared in awe at Patrick's broken body, Arthur thought that the rest of his life would be colored by this moment—the moment that he had inadvertently taken the life of another human being.

*   *   *

"And not only did we have to worry about one of the teachers coming into the room any second—I mean, it *was* between classes," said the female caller to WGRZ Radio 960, "but my . . . big O—"

"You mean your hot fudge sundae," interrupted WGRZ's morning DJ. "Hot fudge sundae" was his pet name for orgasm because he didn't want to offend anyone by actually using the word.

"Uh-huh. My hot fudge sundae," the female caller corrected herself, "seemed to go on for *hours*. I know that's not possible, Alan." The DJ's name was Alan Crocket and he was thought of as the best and ballsiest morning drive-time DJ in New York City. "I know that orgasms . . . oops, I mean hot fudge sundaes, last only a minute or so, maybe not even that long—"

"My producer," Alan cut in, "claims to have had a hot fudge sundae that lasted *five minutes*. Now this is the same woman, you must remember, who claims to have spoken to aliens and who says that, in an earlier life, she was Joan of Arc."

"I think mine lasted five minutes, Alan," said the female caller. "At least five minutes. God, it seemed to go on *forever*."

Alan guffawed. "You girls are lucky. If one of us guys had a hot fudge sundae that lasted that long, we'd be dead."

On the Coast Guard cruiser that had passed beneath Kennedy Whelan's Ford, a young ensign scanned the horizon for signs of the reported rowboat. He saw a yacht named *Stephanie*, which he'd seen more than once in his tour of duty at this station. It was out in all weather, the entire year. And he saw an oil tanker on the horizon. But he saw no abandoned rowboat.

He glanced around at the cruiser's pilot, shivered from the cold breeze that had come up and motioned to the northwest to indicate that they should turn their attentions that way.

Sam asked, "Are you wearing a watch?"

Harry's brow furrowed. He didn't know. He tried pulling back the sleeve of his trench coat. It wouldn't budge. He might as well have been trying to pull back his own skin. He sighed. "I think I am. I don't know."

Sam looked at his left wrist. It was exposed only a little beneath the sleeve of the tweed suit. He held the wrist above his head and peered into the opening between the edges of the sleeve and his wrist. "I've got one," he announced.

"Can you read it?" Harry asked.

"No. But I can see a gold watchband."

"You're sure it's a watch? It could be a bracelet."

"Shit, Harry—I don't wear bracelets." He peered into his suit sleeve again. "You know, I think it's my father's watch. It has to be. I've worn it ever since he died." He dropped his arm. "But it doesn't make any difference if I can't read it."

"Why would you want to know what time it is?" Harry asked.

"I don't know." He shrugged. "Just an idea. Clocks. Watches. Time. Getting caught in time. It was a stab in the dark."

"You're a very intuitive man, aren't you?"

"Intuitive?"

"You think in grand abstractions. I'd assume that that would be a hindrance in your line of work."

Sam looked skeptically at him. "Why do I get the idea that you're making fun of me?"

"I'm not." He wasn't. "And, on second thought,

being a right-brained sort of person would probably be very helpful in your line of work."

"Right-brained?"

"Sure. The kind who absorbs the big picture in one huge chunk and responds to it according to his intuition. He's the kind of person who gets hunches. The kind who can read other people instantly, without knowing *why* or how."

"And that's what I am?"

"Apparently."

The little rowboat was beginning to pitch and roll. It was a very gentle movement, barely noticeable, but Harry noticed it and he grabbed the gunwales. "Shit! Not again!"

Sam said, "It's like this place is alive."

The boat pitched and rolled faster. Small whitecaps formed.

"You know what?" Sam said. "I'll bet we're stuck to this rowboat too. Just like our clothes are stuck to us."

Harry didn't believe it. He shook his head and stiff-armed the gunwales. "If I can grab the sides of the boat like this, I can sure as hell jump *out* of it too."

"You think so? Then try it."

"Hell, no! You try it!"

Sam grinned at him. It was a broad and toothy grin, but tinged with uncertainty.

Harry said, "So go ahead. Have the courage of your convictions."

"I'd like to think about it a moment."

"*Think* about it? What's there to think about? Just latch on to your idea and run with it."

"That's real easy for you to say."

Harry felt like a coward.

Then, in one quick, fluid motion, Sam stood and

leaped from the boat. He hit the frisky blue-green water and was absorbed by it. There was no splash, no turbulence where he went in.

"Oh, Christ!" Harry whispered, and cast about frantically over both sides of the boat. "Dammit to hell!"

Sam reappeared. He was in the same position, at the bow of the boat, that he'd been in before he jumped. And he was still grinning. "I was right," he said. "My God, I was right."

"What did you see?" Harry asked.

"See?"

"When you went in? Did you see anything?"

Sam's grin faded. "Yeah, I did," he said. "I saw the bottom of a boat."

"This boat?"

"I don't think so. It was bigger. It was white."

The ensign on the Coast Guard cruiser motioned frantically for the cruiser's pilot to cut the engines. The pilot obeyed and the cruiser came to a very slow halt in the still, cold water. The ensign called, "Come around, dead slow."

"Did you see something?" the pilot called back.

The ensign nodded. "I think so. A man."

The pilot brought the cruiser around very slowly, aware that if there was a man in the water, the cruiser itself was a hazard to him now.

The ensign ran from port to starboard, looking for the man he'd seen, however briefly, just below the surface. A grinning man. A man with red hair.

Kennedy Whelan's partner, Ian, was pissed off. "Goddammit, Ken, would you get your car phone fixed! I've been trying to reach you for forty-five minutes."

Whelan sat at his desk, put his cup of coffee down

and patted his pocket to see if he had a cigar. He didn't. He frowned. "C'mon, Ian," he grumbled, "you know I need my quiet time." He grinned sardonically.

"Yeah, yeah, don't we all." Whelan had hung his green sports jacket and his overcoat on a coat rack nearby. Ian retrieved them both, handed them to him. "Ken, someone else has gotten their throat cut."

"Wonderful," Whelan said. "Maybe it's the beginning of a trend."

"Yeah, maybe it is," Ian said.

Sydney needed a new tie. The one he'd worn here was beginning to attract attention. There were four diagonal red slashes on it, and although only the desk clerk at the Ritz Carlton had actually said anything, other people had given the tie curious, incredulous looks, as if they weren't sure they were seeing what they *knew* they were seeing—a wide, silver tie with diagonal slashes of blood on it.

He had taken the tie off, folded it neatly, put it in an inside pocket of his black suit jacket and was browsing in the men's department at Bergdorf Goodman's.

A clerk came up and asked if he could be of service.

Sydney was fingering ties on a revolving rack. They were in various tasteful, understated shades and widths. "My good man," Sydney said to the clerk, "these won't do at all. I need a *wide* tie. Don't you have any *wide* ties? And it must be silver. These"—he flipped a few of the tastefully shaded ties with his fingers—"make no statement whatever. Do you understand?"

The clerk was offended, not only by what Sydney was saying but by his odd smell too. "Perhaps Woolworth's could be of greater service to you, sir. Or Kmart, perhaps."

"Are those establishments close by?" Sydney asked.

The clerk grimaced and said, "I'm sure they're close enough," and then fluttered away.

Sydney thought, He's next.

Here's how it works:

Each package will carry a FREE 10-DAY EXAMINATION
privilege. At the end of that time, if you decide
to keep your books, simply pay the low invoice price
of $11.25, no shipping or handling charges added.
HOME DELIVERY IS ALWAYS FREE!
There's no minimum number of books to buy,
and you may cancel at any time.

AND AS A CHARTER MEMBER, YOUR FIRST THREE-BOOK SHIPMENT IS TOTALLY FREE! IT'S A BARGAIN YOU CAN'T BEAT!

✂ CUT HERE

- -

Mail to: Leisure Horror Book Club, P.O. Box 6613, Edison, NJ 08818-6613

YES! I want to subscribe to the Leisure Horror Book Club. Please send
my 3 FREE BOOKS. Then, every other month I'll receive the three newest
Leisure Horror Selections to preview FREE for 10 days. If I decide to
keep them, I will pay the Special Members Only discounted price of just
$3.75 each, a total of $11.25. This saves me between $3.72 and $6.72
off the bookstore price. There are no shipping, handling or other charges
There is no minimum number of books I must buy and I may cancel the
program at any time. In any case, the 3 FREE BOOKS are mine to keep—
at a value of between $14.97 and $17.97. Offer valid only in the USA.

NAME:_____

ADDRESS:_____

    CITY:_____ STATE:_____

    ZIP:_____ PHONE:_____

LEISURE BOOKS, A Division of Dorchester Publishing Co., Inc.

A Stranger's Dreams

Chapter Twenty-three

Amelia watched sullenly as a heavyset, bearded man in his mid-forties, dressed in a Ren and Stimpy T-shirt and a pair of white boxer shorts, trudged from the lake. He looked confused, at first, though only marginally so. It was as if he'd merely gotten on the wrong bus and wasn't sure where the next stop was.

Reluctantly, Amelia waved at him. He caught sight of her, hesitated, waved back. He was a good fifty yards away from where she sat, on her park bench. "Where the hell am I?" he called.

Amelia sighed. Silver Lake was being overrun. She stood, made her way down a set of cement steps to the beach and waited at the bottom for him to reach her.

When he did, he extended his hand. She shook it and said, "My name's Amelia, and I guess I'm Silver Lake's official welcoming committee." She attempted a congenial smile, but it came off badly.

"Jack," said the heavyset man.

Suddenly, they heard a scream.

Amelia jerked her head toward it. Jack did too. "I guess it ain't quite as peaceful here as it looks," he said.

Another scream. Louder. As if someone were in incredible agony.

Kennedy Whelan could barely resist the urge to poke his finger into the gaping wound in Jack South's throat.

From behind him, Ian said, "I don't understand why a grown man would wear a T-shirt like that. What is it—a couple of cartoon characters?" There was a lot of blood on the T-shirt and the colorful imprinting was obscured.

Whelan nodded, eyes still on South's wound. "Yeah," he said. "Cartoons."

South's apartment was a mess. Beer cans littered the place, ashtrays overflowed with cigarette butts, the gray wall-to-wall carpeting was splattered with all kinds of stains—where it wasn't stained with South's blood—and the windows were cloudy with grit. The smell in the place was a noxious mixture of sweat, beer, cigarette smoke and, underlying all of this, an odd, cloying odor that stung the nostrils.

Ian sniffed the air. "Smell that, Ken?"

"I'd rather not," Whelan said, and reached toward South's wound.

"You know what it reminds me of? It reminds me of being in school. Second grade. Miss Fisher's art class."

Whelan glanced around at him, finger poised over South's wound. "Miss Fisher's art class smelled like beer?"

"No. Not the beer smell. That other smell. Like clay."

"Yeah, well, I don't smell nothin' but beer."

There were a number of people gathered around the late Viola Pennypacker's cottage. Amelia had given the cottage to Freely, which had pleased her. "What a gorgeous little house," she'd said.

The people gathered there seemed very concerned. Leonard, who was dressed in olive-green Speedos— he was always dressed in olive-green Speedos— turned to Amelia as she and Jack approached and said, "There appears to be something very wrong here."

June Alexander, standing nearby, turned to Amelia as well. "A lot of pain, I would think, Amelia," she said.

"Pain?" Amelia said. The idea of actual pain here, in her idyllic little community, was ridiculous. No, it was obvious that Anna Freely had at last accepted the bald and distressing fact that she—like Amelia herself, and like this man who called himself Jack, and like the others who had trudged up from the lake recently—was dead, and she was simply reacting to that fact. With tears.

The old woman who called herself Gilly looked at Jack South and said, "Who's this, Amelia?"

"A visitor," Amelia answered.

"One of many, it seems," Gilly replied petulantly.

Amelia gave her a curious look—Gilly was showing some signs of independence and ill temper. That was unlike her, and it took Amelia by surprise.

Amelia went up the little flight of porch steps to Viola Pennypacker's screen door and knocked.

"Anna?" she called, and heard only weeping from within the house.

She sensed someone just behind her, on the porch, turned her head and looked. Jack South grinned at her. "I don't know where I am or how the hell I got here," he said.

"Later," Amelia said, and pointed at the group of people gathered at the bottom of the steps. "Wait down there. This is personal."

Jack nodded enthusiastically. "Personal. Sure. No problem," he said, and went and joined the group. They moved away from him, as if he were an unwelcome intruder, and this too took Amelia by surprise.

She knocked again on Anna's door, but got only agonized weeping in response.

She opened the door and stepped inside.

Freely sat in shadow in a rocking chair across the small front room. She had stopped weeping as soon as Amelia entered the house.

Amelia said, "Is there a problem?"

Freely answered at once, "Yes. I believe that there is."

Amelia sighed. "I'm sorry. I know personally how ... agonizing it is to face up to the face of ... one's own death."

Anna shook her head. "No. I accepted my death some time ago. And I was dealing with it. This is a wonderful little community you've put together, and I saw myself spending lots of time here." She sat forward in the rocking chair. She was still in shadow. "No, Amelia," she went on, voice trembling. "What I've discovered, what has become very clear to me in these past few minutes, is that I am dying—*really* dying." She stood and moved halfway across the room, into the light.

Amelia gasped.

"Shit, Harry," Sam shouted over the white noise of the wind and waves, "you don't need to hold on. There's nothing to worry about." Sam was sitting at the bow of the little boat. He had his fingers laced over his stomach.

But Harry, despite what he *knew*, gripped the little boat's gunwales as if his very existence depended on it and closed his eyes tightly. Which meant that he wasn't able to see Sam flickering, like a light going rapidly on and off, as the wind and waves tossed him from the boat, into the great, airy ocean, and as the powers-that-be, whatever *they* were, put him back into the boat at once, because it was, after all, a part of him and he was a part of it.

Much of Freely looked as if she were made out of dots, the way a newspaper photograph is made out of dots. Her hand: a dozen irregularly shaped gray dots. Her midsection: gray dots. Her head, her right pajama leg, her right foot, her nose, cheeks, lips: all dots. The rest of her was whole. Her green eyes, the creamy white skin of her forehead, her flowing, auburn hair, the area above her cheekbones, her left foot.

Amelia said breathlessly, "What in the hell is happening to you?"

Freely's voice crackled, as if her throat too were disintegrating. "I'm dying, as I said."

"But that's impossible—"

"Because I'm already dead?" She laughed quickly, harshly. "Clearly, Amelia, you're using a term that is not operative here. It may have been operative on . . .

the other side. But not here. I would think you'd have figured that out by now. I didn't think you were a stupid woman." She said this with ill-disguised anger. "You know what I thought, after I'd come here? I thought, Isn't this incredible! Isn't this wonderful! A whole new existence. A new beginning. New people to meet, amazing new places to go and marvelous things to see. But that's not the way it's turning out, is it? I'm dying, Amelia! I'm dying *here*, because I'm *alive* here! And this time, I won't get a second chance. I *know* that."

Amelia knew it too. She could see that it was true. She wanted to reach out to the woman, hold her, assure her that everything would be all right. But she stayed where she was, as if what was happening to Freely was somehow contagious. She said, "But . . . why is this happening to you? Why didn't it happen to me?"

"Who knows? Maybe because this place, this little community and these people all constitute *your* dream, not mine. And how can we live inside a stranger's dreams?"

Amelia didn't know what to say.

Freely slumped back into the rocking chair.

Amelia stared at her for a long moment, then announced, "We'll leave."

Freely chuckled grimly. "How can we do that?"

"I don't know." She cast about for an idea. "Harry's car."

"Harry?"

"My husband . . . former husband. He's got his car here. We'll get in it . . . all of us, you and the others— and we'll leave. I'll take you away from Silver Lake."

* * *

Sam asked, "Do you really think that your Sydney is the first one to go over?"

"I hadn't thought about it," Harry answered tersely. The ocean was calm, but he still gripped the gunwales and kept his eyes closed tightly. "I really hadn't thought about it, Sam. I'd rather not think about it!"

"You can open your eyes," Sam told him. "There's nothing to see." He chuckled. "Do you know how ludicrous you look? Trench coat, black fedora, snub-nosed .38. Mr. Macho PI, and you're acting like a three-year-old who's getting on a roller coaster for the first time."

"Snub-nosed .38?" Harry said.

"Sure. It's what you were pointing at me back in the village. And there it is now."

Harry opened his eyes and looked down at himself. His trench coat was open and he could see the gun peeking out at him from its shoulder holster. "Good Lord," he whispered. "My coat . . ." he said. "It was buttoned."

"Yeah? So?"

"So, it was buttoned, now it's unbuttoned. Sam, are you turning stupid on me?" He sighed. "Sam, I couldn't even pull my coat sleeve back to look at my watch before. Now my coat's unbuttoned. How did *that* happen?"

"I don't know. The storm?"

Harry hesitated, then grabbed hold of the gun and pulled. It stayed put. "Shit!" he muttered.

"Do you really think it's important?" Sam asked.

"Of course it's important." He gave Sam a quick once-over. "How about you? Are you exactly the same as you were before the storm?"

Sam held up his arms, looked at his legs, his torso. "I think so."

"I think so too. Look at you. Even your hair is unruffled."

"Yours looks wet," Sam said.

Harry put his fingers through his hair. It was like putting his fingers through briars, because the hair didn't move. "Is it?" he said.

"Well, it *looks* wet. So does your coat."

"Yours doesn't."

Sam looked at himself again. "You're right."

Harry leaned forward as if to speak confidentially. "Sam, I crossed over. I think I crossed over. Or, at least, I *began* to cross over."

"I think you did too. But why?"

Harry shook his head in confusion. "I'm not sure. What was . . . different about us? What *is* different about us?"

Sam looked at him a moment, sized up the situation. Then he said, "Well, Harry, you're a little taller. Not much taller. An inch, maybe. You're a few years older. You said you were forty-eight. I'm forty-four. You died accidentally. I didn't. I was murdered—"

"Oh?"

Sam nodded. "It's a long story. Some other time."

"Sure."

"And—I'm not being judgmental about this, believe me—but you appear to be a wimp when it comes to water, Harry—"

"That's it," Harry cut in. "And you're right. I'm afraid. I'm *fearful*." He smiled.

Sam's face lit up. "And what," he said, "is more mortal than *fear?* That's it. That's the key."

Harry sat back. He looked suddenly glum. "Maybe, maybe not."

"Why not?"

"Because it still doesn't explain how Sydney got over."

"Did you ever think that there may be more than one road to Cleveland, Harry?"

"Why would we want to go to Cleveland?"

"It was a figure of speech. Jeez!"

Little whitecaps appeared on the calm ocean. "Dammit to hell, here we go again!" Harry said.

Chapter Twenty-four

Sydney was very single-minded. Money, power and murder were what interested him. He didn't think about the weather, or the plight of the whales, or what the latest fashion trends were. He thought about money, power and murder. He thought about the acquisition of money, which would give him power, and about the act of murder, because it piqued his libido. He didn't equate sex with murder. For Sydney, murder *was* sex. He did not stop on the street to watch a beautiful woman pass by. He stopped on the street to think about what a satisfying thing it would be to end this person's life or that person's life. Male or female, young or old, ill or well, it didn't matter.

He had been waiting for several hours for the Bergdorf Goodman's men's department clerk to appear, and he was becoming impatient. He looked at his watch: 5:30. He scowled.

"It's my cat," he heard. He looked up. A woman

was standing in front of him. She was thin and hatchet-faccd, and her black hair hung in greasy strips down to her skinny shoulders. She was dressed shabbily. "My cat is all the powers of darkness!" she proclaimed, hand raised, index finger pointing at the gray sky. She had a gleam in her small eyes that Sydney liked. "My cat has come with his devils and minions to claim spaces on the earth and he is *brown* and *white* and bears three toes on both feet. He breathes clams!"

Sydney smiled crookedly at her.

The woman smiled crookedly back, then skittered off.

The Bergdorf Goodman men's department clerk, just coming out of the store, passed her, apparently didn't notice her, then looked Sydney in the eye and apparently failed to notice him too.

Sydney followed him.

"But I just got here," Jack South protested. "Why do I have to leave?"

Amelia took him by the arm and ushered him away from the late Viola Pennypacker's cottage and toward Harry's monster Buick, parked not far away. "Because, if you don't leave," she said, "you'll die."

Jack thought this was very strange. "Is there something toxic here? Is that what you're telling me? Was this place built on a chemical dump or something? God, Love Canal and . . . now this place. What did you call it? Silver Lake? Maybe *that's* why the lake is silver. Jesus, how awful."

"Yeah," Amelia said, "that's why you have to leave. A chemical dump."

The group that had gathered outside Viola Pennypacker's cottage was following them, even though

Amelia had wanted them to stay where they were. It was all right, she thought. Obviously she'd given them a little more free will than she'd supposed, which meant that they could act with some limited independence. That wasn't so bad. It made them less predictable. They'd be more fun to have around, now that it was clear that Harry—if he ever returned—wouldn't be able to stay.

"Where are we going?" Jack South asked, as Amelia opened the passenger door of the Buick and nodded for him to get in.

"I don't know," she answered. "I'm not sure. Wait here."

"Wait here? Why?"

"It's safer."

He got in. "Maybe I could listen to the radio while I'm waiting?"

"The radio? Sure. Turn it on."

"I can't do that without the keys."

"Oh, shit," Amelia whispered. She hadn't thought that she'd need the keys.

"Oh, wait a minute," Jack said. "Here they are. In the ignition. Bad habit to leave your keys in the ignition."

Amelia breathed a sigh of relief. "Yes," she said. "My husband's always doing that. He's forgetful sometimes."

Jack turned on the ignition. He smiled. Music poured out of the car speakers with the slightest turn of the tuning knob.

"This is great," he said. "I didn't know there were so many stations to listen to."

Amelia's brow furrowed. "I didn't either," she said. She touched Jack on the shoulder. "I'll be back shortly. Don't leave the car, okay?"

"Okay," Jack said.

Sleepeasy

* * *

The men's department clerk for Bergdorf Goodman's was thinking about his evening meal. Chicken divan would be nice, he decided. Or veal marsella. He was hungry. His stomach growled. He put his hand on it and whispered, "Quiet, there," because he was afraid it would embarrass him.

His name was Clive. He was thirty-seven years old, had never been married, lived with a parakeet he had named "My Friend" and both his parents were dead, which was fine with him because they had been a chore to have around, always after him to "get married," "have a relationship," "make something of yourself other than as someone who sells ties."

But he did more than sell ties, of course. He sold all sorts of men's clothing. Quality clothing. Clothing that would last. Clothing that said something important about the wearer. Oh, we are more than just our inner selves, aren't we? he maintained. We cannot run around naked, as appealing as that might be to some. We have to put on the *appearance* of taste and quality, because that is the way the world judges us.

Clive himself was very well dressed. He spent half of his salary on his clothes.

He wasn't aware that Sydney was following him. Not because Sydney was particularly skillful at following people. He wasn't. It was not in his nature to be covert. His kind of murder was certainly not covert. Clive wasn't aware of Sydney because Clive was so self-involved. If there were other people on the street, it was of little consequence to him unless they made it difficult for him to pass. If that happened, he merely lowered his head a little—as if to use it like a battering ram—and said firmly, "Excuse me! Let me by!" It usually worked.

Sydney wasn't aware of Clive's self-involvement. He couldn't have cared less if Clive turned around, saw him and guessed what was in his head. Indeed, Sydney would have liked that. It would have made the chase, and the kill, much more interesting. But right now, what most interested Sydney was doing away with this toad who had offended him. Quickly. But painfully.

Clive turned toward Fifth Avenue. He was looking for a cab. He never took the subway or the buses. Too smelly. Only lower-class people used subways and buses.

He saw a cab with its VACANT sign up and raised his hand to hail it.

A huge, meaty hand grabbed his wrist. He gasped. What was this? Someone had the temerity to accost him on a crowded city street. . . .

He felt another meaty hand around his throat.

He heard, "My God, look at what that man is doing!"

And, "Hey, you, stop that!"

He felt his windpipe collapse. He gasped for air.

He heard, "He *killed* that man!"

"Yeah," came the reply. "C'mon. Our dinner reservations are for six-fifteen."

Clive crumpled to the pavement and gasped for air that wouldn't come.

His stomach churned. Christ, he was going to throw up. What an indignity! The vomit came, but stopped halfway up his throat, unable to pass his collapsed windpipe.

*   *   *

Water surrounded him. A sandy beach lay ahead and he trudged toward it.

An angry-looking man in olive-green Speedos stood at the shore. "Go away!" he screamed. "You can't stay here!"

Chapter Twenty-five

Amelia couldn't find the two picnickers. She hoped they had merely wandered off, still in search of a sandy beach, but knew in her heart that that was not what had happened to them.

She also couldn't find Barrow, Freely's boyfriend. She had put him in with Mrs. Alexander—after some protest from the woman, which surprised Amelia— but now Mrs. Alexander had no idea where Barrow was. "You know, dear," she said—it was the first time that Mrs. Alexander had called her "dear" and Amelia didn't know what she thought of it—"when I last saw him, he was very . . . still. And I can tell you this too—he wasn't all there."

"Wasn't all there?"

"That's right. He wasn't much more than his chest and legs—and his head, of course, and parts of his arms. I asked him what was wrong, but he couldn't speak, apparently. It's such a shame." Her tone was light and casual. She might as well have been talking about a recipe that hadn't turned out right.

"And where was he then?" Amelia asked.

"In the back bedroom, where you told me to put him, dear. I went there to ask him to leave. I don't like him. None of us likes these people."

"You were going to ask him to leave?" Amelia was shocked. Where had Mrs. Alexander gotten the idea that she could do something like that?

"Yes, dear. He's not one of us, is he?"

"Us?"

"Us, yes." She grinned as if she were bursting to tell a secret.

"And you're saying that you went back there, to tell him to leave, and . . ."

"And he wasn't all there. That's right. And now I think he's not there at all. Like the Cheshire Cat." Another secretive grin. Broader, but with an added touch of malice. "Now, I think that, *poof*, he's gone. Like all these intruders will be!"

So, unable to locate Barrow, Amelia found Sydney's other victim—the well-dressed man named Morgan—coaxed Freely out of Viola Pennypacker's house, after much effort and cajoling, and piled the two of them into the backseat of Harry's monster Buick. She argued for a few minutes with Jack about the radio: Amelia wanted it off, Jack insisted that it stay on. Amelia lost the argument, only because she didn't want to waste any more time.

"There's nothing to worry about," she told them all, as she put the Buick in gear and roared off down the village's main street, toward what she was convinced were its boundaries.

Meanwhile, Clive stood a hundred feet out in Silver Lake, unable to move because Leonard was shaking his fist and unloading an incredible volley of curses and threats at him.

The latest storm was over, the ocean and sky were calm and Harry's black fedora lay in the bottom of the boat. He reached over to retrieve it. It wouldn't budge. "Dammit!" he said. "I liked that hat."

"Conjure up a new one," Sam told him.

"I think I did all the conjuring I was allowed back in Silver Lake, Sam."

"Too bad."

"How about you?" Harry said.

"I didn't know I *could* conjure. Maybe I really couldn't. Shit, what did I know? One minute I'm walking down a nice tree-lined street in Boston and the next minute I'm fifty feet in the air, rammed by a big, fat mother of a Lincoln. Then, wham, I'm ten years old again—"

"Ten years old?"

"Uh-huh. I died. Then I was ten years old, playing cowboys and Indians. It was a great time in my life and I guess I was being allowed to relive it."

"Nothing like that happened to me," Harry said. It was clear from his tone that he felt cheated.

Sam said, "If you're asking me to explain *why* it didn't happen to you . . ."

"No, I'm not. I'm sorry. I think there were mitigating factors. I think the fact that I died with a lot of . . . baggage in tow—"

"Your wife?"

"My feelings for her. Yes. I don't think we had the best of relationships. I wasn't aware of it at the time. I am now." He sighed.

"My condolences," Sam said.

"Yeah, sure," Harry said. "But, you know, as bad

as it was, as combative as it was, I think she loved me. I know I loved her. Hell, I still do."

"Let me tell you what I think," Sam said. "I think that if *you* manage to go back over to the other side, then I'll be dragged along on your coattails."

Harry didn't know if he liked the ham-handed way that Sam had changed the topic of conversation. He shrugged. "It's a theory. I mean, I dragged you to Silver Lake, didn't I?"

"Apparently."

"But that still doesn't give us any idea how I'm going to go over. It reminds me of something Barbara used to say: 'If we had ham, we could have ham and cheese. If we had cheese.' "

"And now that we're tossing clichés around, how about this one: 'The later it gets, the later it gets.' "

"Meaning?"

"Meaning that each time we have one of these little storms, you're bound to become less and less fearful. And I think we've agreed that that's our ticket to the other side. Your fear."

Harry thought about this and nodded sullenly. "You're right." He shook his head. "Sam, I think we're stuck here. Goddammit, I think we're stuck here."

Sam smiled. Not if I can help it! he told himself.

Kennedy Whelan was getting sick of being a homicide detective. Nearly thirty years at it and what did he have to show for his trouble? A few dismal possessions and an army of the dead pleading with him to find their murderers. Because not every killer is brought to justice, of course. The man who merely decides—for whatever twisted reason—to off a stranger one rainy night leaves almost no trail at all.

181

And the contract killer is usually thorough at covering his ass. The only homicides that had a reasonable expectation of being solved were those that resulted from family disputes. Wife shoots husband. Husband strangles wife. Son kills mother, father, sister. Good, clean, straightforward murders. And justifiable sometimes too. Who could blame a wife for slicing up an errant, abusive husband, for instance? There was little fulfillment in bringing those people to justice.

As he bent over Clive's body, he said to his partner, Ian, "His damn throat is crushed. Jesus." In all his years as a homicide detective, Whelan had seen few murder victims with their throats crushed. It took a massive effort to crush the fibrous cartilage that comprised the windpipe.

"I saw it happen," Whelan heard. He looked. A blond woman in her early twenties, dressed in blue jeans and red T-shirt, stood nearby.

"Did you?" Whelan asked.

She nodded enthusiastically. "He"—she pointed stiffly at Clive—"didn't have no chance at all. Poor snot."

Whelan stared at her a moment. This was too good to be true—a witness to a street killing. "And your name is?"

"Jimmy."

"Jimmy what?"

"Jimmy Dean."

Whelan smiled. "I assume that's your stage name?"

She shook her head and frowned, as if offended. "It ain't no stage name. It's my real name."

"Jimmy Dean. Okay, tell me what you saw, Jimmy."

"I saw it happen. I told you."

"Yes, I know. But what I'd like you to do is describe the killer for me. Can you do that?"

She nodded. "Sure. He was big. And he was bald."

"And?"

"I can't tell you nothing else. He was big and bald. You're lookin' at a big bald guy chokin' some little snot, how much are you gonna see?"

Whelan frowned, took a cigar out of his pocket, put it back. Maybe he'd really think seriously about quitting.

"Tell me what you're afraid of," Sam said.

"You mean, besides the water?" Harry said. He thought a moment, then went on, "Tidal waves. They're very high on my fear list, though I've never seen one. Just the idea of all that raw *power*..." He shuddered, then continued. "But I guess that doesn't count, does it? Tidal waves are made of water." A moment's silence. "Dying painfully is high on my list too. But that probably doesn't count anymore either." He looked confusedly at Sam. "Why do you ask?"

"Just to make conversation," Sam told him. It was a lie.

"Oh," Harry said.

"So, go ahead. Tidal waves, painful death. What else?"

"I don't know. Being blind. That's a common fear, isn't it?"

"I think so."

"But I don't mean simply being unable to see. That's bad enough. No, what really scares me is being in a place that's strange, a place I've never been before, *and* being blind. Reaching out to touch what's around me and not knowing what the hell it is I'm touching."

"I understand," Sam said glumly.

"Something wrong?"

"Not really. I just thought . . . never mind. Anything else? Another fear? People who leer? People who sneer?"

"Huh? Why are you rhyming?"

Sam was surprised. "Am I? I wasn't aware of it. I'm sorry, there's certainly no glory . . . in rhyming. It's a habit I slip into from time to time. I like to rhyme." He took a deep breath. "Fears. Any other fears?"

Harry stared at him a moment, then said, "Uh-huh. Being ingested."

"Ingested. You mean eaten?"

"Yeah. Being chomped down on by a shark or a crocodile, and then being *eaten*. And it doesn't matter if that first bite does you in either. What really matters is that you—the sum of God's powers, the pinnacle of the creative forces in the universe, a thing with a soul, and emotions, and family, and feelings and thoughts about the future—are going to end up inside some other creature's *intestines*. You're going to become crocodile shit!"

Sam shuddered. "Jesus, I see what you mean. It's enough to make me turn green." It was the truth.

"And thanks a hell of a lot for making me talk about it," Harry said. "What I really need out here is to be discussing my deepest fears."

"Yes," Sam said, smiling secretively, "I know."

184

Getting the Job Done

Chapter Twenty-six

"Do you know where we're going?" Jack South asked.

But Amelia hadn't heard him above the loud rock music blaring from the Buick's twelve-speaker sound system. She reached over, turned the radio down and asked him to repeat himself.

"Where are we going?" he said again.

"Yes," Morgan asked from the backseat. "Where are we going?"

Freely stayed quiet.

They had just passed Chelmsford Road—which Amelia had never heard of and was sure wasn't one of her creations—and they were surrounded by fields of tall grass and sunflowers. The road had suddenly become narrow and rutted, and they were being bounced around like marshmallows.

"This is very pretty," Jack South said.

"I think we're going east," Amelia said.

The strangled voice of Freely said from the back-seat, "She doesn't know where the piss we're going."

Morgan asked, "How the hell can you tell which direction we're traveling in if there's no sun?"

"Sure there's a sun," Jack South told him. "Look at it out there. Sunlight."

"Idiot!" Morgan hissed. "When I say there's no sun, I don't mean there's no sun*light*, I mean there's no *sun!*"

Jack opened his window, craned his head out, looked around. "You're right. There's no sun. Where's the fucking sun?"

Amelia turned the radio back on to divert Jack's attention.

Freely croaked from the backseat, "There's no sun because we're all dead, Jack. Some of us are more dead than others, of course."

Jack looked around at her. "Did you say something about being dead?"

"For Christ's sake, isn't it obvious? *Look* at me!"

"I am, I am! And?"

Amelia brought the car to a stop at a crossroads. Straight ahead, the road narrowed further and she could see that it ended not far off. To the left, it widened. To the right, there was more of the same narrow, rutted road. They were still surrounded by fields of tall grass and sunflowers.

She took a left.

How easy was this going to be? Sam wondered.

"Lost in thought?" Harry asked.

"Yes," Sam answered.

"About what?"

Sam grinned a little, then answered, "Possibilities."

"What sorts of possibilities?"

"All sorts. I think there are probably billions . . . no, *trillions* of possibilities."

Harry smiled. "There are probably as many possibilities as there are combinations of molecules and electrons."

"Sure," Sam said. "At least that many." An indefinable speck on the horizon—or what passed for the horizon, here—caught his attention. He smiled quickly—so, his idea was working!—and focused on it.

Harry craned his head around. "Do you see something?"

"I don't know. I think so," Sam answered tentatively.

"Yes," Harry said. "I do too. What do you think it is? Maybe it's a ship." This seemed to cheer him.

"It doesn't look like a ship," Sam said.

"How can you tell at this distance?" Harry countered.

The speck on the horizon grew slowly as they watched. It took on a shape—bulbous, like a weather balloon—and a color—black. A black, bulbous thing against the blue-green horizon.

"I think it's a ship," Harry declared happily. "I think that we've crossed over—Lord knows how— and that's a ship and it's going to . . . rescue us."

"*Rescue* us?"

Harry grimaced. "Yes, I suppose that does sound ludicrous, doesn't it?"

"Harry, I'm sorry, but I don't think it's a ship."

"What else could it be?"

They both watched as the thing drew closer to the little rowboat, until, at last, it became clear to Harry that Sam was right.

"It's not a ship," he said glumly.

189

Sam agreed.

"For Christ's sake . . ." His voice was edging in on panic. The thing had closed to within a mile or so of the little rowboat and he could see that it was huge, bulbous, black and wild-eyed. It moved leadenly and inexorably toward them over the calm water. "For Christ's sake, Sam, look at that thing! My God, it's *alive!*"

"Where did it come from?" Sam asked, though he knew only too well.

Harry was astonished. "Who gives a shit where it came from? For God's sake, row!" He reached frantically for the oars. Sam reached too, got them first and began to row hard.

Harry looked back at the huge, wild-eyed creature bearing down on them.

The thing's mouth opened.

Harry screamed.

Sam screamed—if only for effect—and thought, That's close enough, because the thing was only a stone's throw away and it towered over the little boat like a black tidal wave, its gummy mouth—and apparently endless rows of pointed teeth—opened wide.

Harry screamed again.

That's far enough! Sam thought. Why in the hell wasn't it following his directions? *He* had created it, after all. *He* had conjured it up, because what was more mortal than *fear?*

The thing pushed the water ahead of it as it moved, wild eyes intent on its victims, gummy mouth salivating.

It swamped the little boat and the boat turned over.

Harry screamed again.

Sam screamed, though not solely for effect this time.

That's enough, enough, enough! he thought frantically.

And found that he was falling through the blue-green and airy ocean.

He caught sight of Harry, far off, falling too and being pursued by the black, wild-eyed, bulbous thing that he, Sam, had conjured up and now could not control. He could hear Harry screaming. It was continuous, ragged, distant. And very fearful. Sam yelled as he fell, "Forgive me, my friend! I had no idea what the hell I could do!"

191

Chapter Twenty-seven

Sydney sat very still in his suite at the Ritz Carlton. The lights were off. The TV was off. The shades were drawn. The rooms were in near darkness.

Sydney wasn't sleeping, though. Nor was he resting, or taking some "quiet time." Sydney was existing. When he wasn't killing or involved in the acquisition of power and money, he merely sat.

He had no thoughts per se. The memories of his recent murders swam around in his head like bits of muck in a dirty fishbowl and he enjoyed them.

But as he sat, he felt a little discomfort too. It wasn't pain exactly. It wasn't a headache, a backache, a toothache. It was pressure, as if something unseen were tugging gently but insistently on him from all sides at once.

* * *

Dammit, Amelia thought, more fucking sunflowers!

"Look at all the fucking sunflowers!" Morgan said from the backseat.

"And what *I* want to know," Jack called—head stuck out the monster Buick's window—"is where do all these sunflowers come from if there's no fucking sun?"

"Isn't *that* a good question?" shouted Freely, sitting next to Morgan in the backseat. "And you can bet your ass that our indomitable Captain Amelia doesn't know the answer."

Amelia had the Buick's accelerator pedal to the floor and the car's big engine was pulling them over the rutted road at close to ninety-five miles an hour. She had seen no other cars, no people, no animals, only the road and the fields and the sunflowers—which seemed to nod in a friendly way as they passed—so she thought that her speed didn't matter, and she was getting a kick out of it anyway.

She wasn't getting a kick out of Freely's attitude. The woman was turning into a real bitch. Even if she was . . . dying, it was no reason to make life unpleasant for everyone around her.

Amelia chanced a quick glance at her, before returning her gaze to the road. *Huh?* she thought. She looked once more. "Freely," she said. "Good Lord, you're whole!"

"My hole?" Freely snapped back. "What is that, some sexual slur?"

Amelia sighed. "No, no, no. I mean, you're . . . entire. You're all there."

193

"I am?" She looked down at herself. "Jesus, I *am!* How in the hell did that happen?"

"My guess," Amelia said, "is that it happened because we got out of Silver Lake." She let off a bit on the accelerator pedal. Suddenly, and inexplicably, excessive speed had lost its appeal.

"At last," Freely proclaimed, "you're *right* about something."

"Bitch," Amelia whispered.

"Look there!" Jack said. He was leaning out the window, pointing straight ahead. The fields of sunflowers ended not far away and buildings were visible.

Amelia let off further on the accelerator, so the car was barely crawling.

"What the fuck's the problem?" Morgan shouted. "And turn down that damned music."

Amelia turned it off.

"Hey!" Jack said.

"Just for a moment," Amelia said, and peered through the windshield. "I don't like the feel of this."

"The feel of *what?*" Morgan barked.

Amelia wasn't sure. The buildings ahead—halfway to the horizon—looked innocent enough. Square, gray, apparently made of cinder block. They were certainly ugly, but there was nothing overtly menacing about them.

"Step on it!" Morgan ordered. "This car's too damned hot!"

Why is everyone so testy? Amelia wondered. Was it the heat? The road that cut through the field of sunflowers certainly seemed hotter than it should.

"Jack, could you roll up your window, please," she said.

"Roll up the window? Sure. You going to turn on the air-conditioning?" He pressed the button for the power window. Amelia found the electronic hum of the window closing oddly comforting.

"Yes," she answered, "I'm going to turn on the air-conditioning," and she did. Cold air flowed into the car almost at once.

"Good fucking idea!" Morgan bellowed. "Jesus, I'm sweating back here!"

"It's on, it's on," Amelia told him.

They were very close to the cinder-block buildings now and Amelia could see what had made her instinctively uncomfortable about them. They looked like prisons. Small, barred windows. Sturdy, metal doors.

She stopped the car a hundred yards away. She could see no people, no sign of habitation.

"What the hell is this?" Morgan asked.

"It looks like Attica," Freely said.

"Or Leavenworth," Jack said.

"It's someone's twisted fantasy," Amelia told them, and thought that whoever indulged in such fantasies wasn't someone she wanted to meet.

"Why are we stopped?" Jack asked. "Let's get a move on."

"She doesn't have any idea where we're going, let alone where we are," Freely said. "I think she's doing the correct thing."

Amelia glanced at her. "Thanks."

"Sisters, right?" Freely said, and grinned back.

Amelia smiled uneasily at her. The whole *sisters*

idea had always seemed a little . . . constipating. "Sure," she said. "Sisters."

"All right, all right," Morgan chimed in, "that's enough of the female-bonding crap. Are we going to move or not? We can't simply stay here."

"I've got to think," Amelia said.

"About what?" Morgan asked. "If you don't like this place, then we drive on. We go somewhere you *do* like. Somewhere all of us like."

Amelia looked at him. "I don't think that's in the cards."

"Oh, you don't." He sighed. "Okay, I guess I understand that—"

"You do?" Jack cut in.

"Who's that?" Freely said.

Amelia, who had been looking at Morgan, turned to the road again. A man was standing fifty yards off, in the middle of the road. He wore what looked like a black uniform with yellow insignias on the arms. His stance was very erect and he held what looked like a bazooka.

"Shit!" Jack whispered.

"I say we turn around," Morgan offered. "This guy doesn't look friendly."

"Agreed," Amelia said, and put the car in reverse.

Just then the man in the road lifted the bazooka to his shoulder, as if preparing to fire.

Amelia floored the accelerator.

Harry's feet felt wet and his head hurt. He reached to touch his head and his fingers hit a wall behind him. "Shit!" he whispered.

He couldn't see and at first he thought it was because he was blind, which gave him a little rush of panic. Then his eyes adjusted to the light and he realized that he was in a small, dank, windowless room. Light filtered into the room beneath what looked like a door a dozen feet in front of him. He could hear people talking loudly outside. He listened for a moment and, though he couldn't make out any single words, he got the idea that the loud talking was not in anger. He could hear other sounds and he guessed that they were the sounds of machines, and that people were talking loudly to make themselves heard over the machines.

He reached carefully toward his head again, avoiding the wall. His head felt wet. He tried to peer at his fingers but with no success, and guessed that the wetness on his fingers was blood.

He pushed himself slowly to his feet—he ached all over, as if he'd done a full day's worth of heavy labor—and trudged toward the door.

Where were his shoes? he wondered. His feet were bare and he was walking through slimy puddles. The place stunk too. Urine, beer. And it was very cold.

He reached through the darkness, found a doorknob, turned it, pushed. The door wouldn't budge. He pulled on the door. It opened. Bright light flooded over him and he raised his arm to his eyes.

"Who the hell is that?" he heard.

"Hey, buddy, what are you doing here?"

He lowered his arm. A half dozen workmen in hard hats stood close by, staring at him.

"Where am I?" he said.

"Where you shouldn't be," one of the workmen answered. "Good God, Mack, this place is going to go down in two hours. What were you doing, sleeping one off in there?"

"No. I don't know. I don't think so." Harry was

very confused. What was this place? How had he gotten here?

"He's bleeding," one of the workmen said.

"You know you're bleeding, Mack?"

Harry reached, felt his head, looked at his fingers. Blood. He looked into the face of a workman with puffy cheeks and small eyes. "What is this place?"

"Huh?" the man said.

"Someone get him out of here," a voice said.

Another workman came forward and took Harry by the arm. "C'mon, buddy."

Harry tried unsuccessfully to shake off the man's grip. "Don't give me no trouble, okay?" the man said.

"Sorry," Harry said.

"We gotta take the stairs, okay? It's a long way down. You think you're up to it?"

The walls of the building were pockmarked with holes. Harry thought he could see the Con Ed building through one of these holes. "This is New York?" he asked, astonished.

"Yeah." The man chuckled. "Where else would they be knocking a building down for Christmas?" This didn't register with Harry. He nodded vaguely and wondered what the hell he was doing in New York City. The last thing he remembered was watching Barbara take one of her nude swims.

The man led him to a flight of cement steps. Harry looked down. "How far up are we?"

"Fifteen stories."

"And we have to walk? There's no elevator?"

"That's right."

"I don't think I'm up to that."

"You sure as hell are," the man said, and chuckled. "*Up* to it, I mean." He chuckled again and guided

Harry to the top of the stairs. "It's the only way outa here. Just be careful. There's ice."

Harry took the first step down, then another. "I'm so tired," he said.

"Yeah, ain't we all!" the man said.

Chapter Twenty-eight

"He vanished!" Jack whispered. "That guy simply vanished."

Amelia hit the brake pedal hard and stared through the windshield. "He did, didn't he?" This was crazy. One moment, the guy's pointing what looks like a bazooka at them and then, when she backs away, he's gone, along with his ugly cinder-block buildings. And they—Morgan, Freely, Jack South and she—are awash in nodding sunflowers and blue-green sky again.

"You know what it reminds me of?" Morgan said from the backseat. "It reminds me of a computer game."

"Yeah," Freely said. "It does."

"You're right," Jack said. "You get to a certain place in a computer game, where you're going to get killed or something, and when you go *backward*, you're all right. Then you go a different way, or you stay where you are, and think about what you oughta do next."

"Because," Freely explained, "the enemy is out of the frame, off the screen."

"This is *not* a computer game," Amelia told them.

"It's not *our* computer game anyway!" Morgan said.

"It's not a computer game at all," Amelia said. "It's . . . What it is . . . is . . ." She cast about for the proper words. Did she even *know* the proper words? she wondered. "What it is," she finished, "is someone else's reality."

"Yeah, like I said," Morgan chuckled, "it's someone's computer game."

Amelia sighed. "Listen, I know what I'm talking about. This is *my* world after all."

"Yours?" Morgan objected. "It's ours too. And everyone else's."

Amelia pursed her lips in annoyance. These people simply didn't understand. Although, on second thought, how could they? They were the recently dead after all. And so they were confused, as she once had been. No one could blame them for not thinking straight. "This is what I'm going to do," she announced.

"Wait a minute," Morgan cut in. "Who died and made you boss?"

Amelia glared at him.

"Yeah," Freely agreed. "Who died and made you boss?"

"Do you think that's *funny?*" Amelia asked, astonished.

"No. Just a damned good question," Morgan answered.

201

"A *fucking* damned good question," Freely chimed in.

Amelia looked at her. "I thought we were sisters?"

Freely shrugged.

She glanced from Morgan to Jack South. "I'm the boss because I've been here longer than any of you and because I know what I'm doing."

"Hah!" Morgan harrumphed.

"And because I've got control of the car," Amelia finished, smiling. "And what I've decided we're going to do is confront the enemy." And with that, she put the car in drive and floored the accelerator.

Within moments, the squat, gray, cinder-block buildings appeared, followed almost instantly by the man with the bazooka. He raised it to his shoulder.

"Get down!" Amelia barked, and stiff-armed the steering wheel.

But nobody got down. All eyes were trained on the man with the bazooka.

Amelia closed her eyes.

When she opened them, the man was jumping out of the way and the bazooka was flying skyward.

She hit the brake and the Buick screeched to a halt. Craning her head around, she saw the man at the side of the road. He was sitting up, massaging his knees. He was in his sixties, she guessed, and he looked hurt, angry and confused.

"I'm sorry," she called. "You looked like you meant business with that . . . weapon of yours."

He glanced at her, then back at his knees. "Well, I *did* mean business, until I figured out that you weren't one of mine. They haven't degenerated to the point where they're actually trying to run me over yet."

Remarkably, she thought she understood what he was talking about.

She glanced around at the ugly gray buildings: there were seven of them and they were all clustered near the road. Beyond, atop a little rise, she could see a nice, two-story, white colonial house with green shutters and a red slate roof. "What is this place?" she asked.

The man looked at her a moment, as if trying to decide whether to answer or not. "I call it Bunker Number Four."

"Oh," she said.

"See," Morgan called from within the car. "I told you it was a computer game."

The man in the roadway shook his head and pushed himself to his feet. He was thin and balding, and his eyes were large, gray and rheumy, as if he spent much of his time in darkness, or asleep. "It's not a computer game," he said. "It's more sophisticated than that."

"Virtual reality then," Jack South called. He was sticking his head out of the passenger window.

The man shrugged. "Reality, virtual reality—who knows? It works, so it *is*."

Shit, Amelia thought. Another philosopher.

The man started walking toward the car. He limped, which gave her a little pang of guilt. "I didn't mean to scare you. You're the first real flesh-and-blood people I've seen in quite a long time. Years, I think. Actually, it's very good to have real people here, although you must realize that you can't stay for long." It was not a threat, merely a statement of fact, and Amelia understood it only too well.

"How long?" she asked.

He was at the rear of the car now. He stopped, put his hand on the fender, as if to steady himself, breathed heavily for a moment and then smiled sheepishly at her. "I don't think I can answer that question," he said. "As I told you, it's been a very long time since I had flesh-and-blood people here. I don't remember how long you're allowed to stay—"

"Allowed?" Morgan said. He was sticking his head out of the rear passenger window. "Allowed by whom?"

Again, the man smiled sheepishly. "Whoever is in charge, I guess. God, maybe."

"That's absurd," Morgan said.

"It's a reflection of his ignorance," Freely said.

"Don't insult the man," Amelia ordered.

"She thinks someone died and made her boss," Jack South said.

Amelia grimaced. "He thinks that's funny."

"It *is* funny," the man said, grinning. "It's very funny." He sighed. "If you want to stay, I'm afraid you'll have to leave in a couple of hours. By then you'll start . . . coming apart—"

"Disintegrating," Freely cut in. She got out of the car and confronted the man with the bazooka. "I know precisely what happens because it happened to me!"

The man said, "Yes. It happened to me too."

Freely backed off. "Really?"

He nodded sullenly. "It was quite an awful experience. Worse than death, and I think we all know how *that* felt. At least with death we knew, right from the beginning, that there was . . . more—"

"Wait just a cotton-pickin' minute," Jack South interrupted. "Everyone here has been talking about death and dying and all that stuff ever since I arrived, and I want to know why. It sounds pretty creepy to me."

All eyes settled pityingly on him.

The man with the bazooka—which was lying on the road not far off—came over and put his hand comfortingly on Jack South's shoulder. Jack looked suspiciously at the man's hand. "You got somethin' on your mind, I can tell," he said.

"Well, son," the man said soothingly, "in point of fact, some of us arrive in this place equipped with certain unalterable truths. And some of us don't."

"I guess I'm one of those that don't," Jack said.

The man nodded. "That does appear to be the case," he said, and then went on to tell Jack what everyone else already knew about themselves, and about Jack.

When he was done, Jack shook his head in disbelief and stared leadenly out of the windshield.

The man with the bazooka, who introduced himself as "Conrad," said, "He'll be all right. They always are. What choice do they have, after all?" Then he invited the rest of the group to his house for lunch.

Jack South stayed in the car.

Harry was barefoot and broke, and he had no idea what he was doing in Manhattan. He was wearing a brown trench coat and a threadbare, gray double-breasted suit, which was warm enough, but no shoes, and his feet were growing numb.

After the workman had deposited him on the first floor of the building that was undergoing demolition, a cop hustled over and ushered Harry off to an area some distance away, where onlookers numbering in the thousands had gathered.

Now Harry was standing at the front of the crowd and wondering what the hell he was going to do without any money or shoes.

"Don't stay here," he heard. He looked about. Who had spoken? he wondered. A fat woman in a black hat stood to his left, but when he looked questioningly

at her she didn't acknowledge him, and he realized
that the voice he'd heard had been the voice of a man
anyway. He looked at a well-dressed, older man
standing to his right. "Excuse me," Harry said to him,
"but did you just say something?"

"No," the man answered curtly, "I didn't," and it
was clear from his tone that he didn't want to be
bothered.

Harry turned a little to look at the people behind
him. None of them looked back.

"Don't stay here," he heard, and realized, with a
little shiver, that the voice seemed to be coming from
within his own head. My God, he thought, I'm going
crazy!

"No," said the voice, "you're not going crazy.
We've got places to go, people to see, investigations
to make. Remember Sydney?"

"But I *must* be crazy," Harry said aloud.

"Shh!" said the well-dressed man beside him, and
he realized that the huge crowd, which had gathered
to watch this building's demolition, was eerily quiet,
as if they were waiting for a birth to happen or a
violin concerto to begin.

"Damned loonies everywhere," muttered the fat
woman standing to his left. "Not even wearing
shoes."

"Shh!" said the well-dressed man.

"Don't you shush me!"

And the voice inside Harry's head chattered on,
"I'm here, my friend, so listen to me/There are lots
better places for you to be."

Harry nodded. He was sure the voice was right.

"I don't know what your problem is," the voice
continued. "Maybe when you made the leap you got
looped, or plooped, don't ask me which,/But it's def-

initely some kind of cosmic glitch./Maybe you fooled someone in authority,/Someone in charge,/Someone large,/Or maybe when you arrive here,/You're alive here./But if you are alive,/It's probably not going to last,/So you'd better do your snooping fast."

"Not going to last?" Harry whispered. Of course he wasn't going to last. No one did. Everyone was mortal. His inner voice was making no sense at all, and speaking to him in rhyme besides. This was not a good sign.

He stepped forward, glanced right and left, and saw no way around the crowd except backward, through it, which didn't appeal to him.

He stepped back again. "What part of Manhattan is this?" he asked the fat woman.

Her chest heaved in annoyance. "Good heavens," she said, "it's Fifty-ninth Street and Sixth Avenue."

"And they're going to blow that building up?" It was a tall building, but not by New York City standards. It stood about twenty stories, he guessed. Much of the glass had been removed.

"No," said the fat woman sarcastically, "we're just here for our health."

"And what if I don't want to stick around?"

"Then that is your business," said the well-dressed man.

Harry could *feel* the crowd behind him. Its mass and weight and anticipation.

The voice in his head said, "This is sick. Thousands of people waiting around to see a building destroyed. People are anarchists at heart. Order doesn't really appeal to them. Just disorder."

"It's only human," Harry said, happy at any rate that the voice had stopped speaking to him in rhyme.

"What they're doing is watching the old give way to the new."

"And he *talks* to himself as well," muttered the fat woman.

"Remember Sydney?" repeated the voice inside Harry's head.

"Sydney?" Harry said. "In Australia?"

"Shhh!" said the fat woman.

"Sydney in Australia?" said the voice in Harry's head. "What the hell are you talking about?"

"It's the capital of Australia. Sydney," Harry answered.

"If you're going to talk to yourself," said the well-dressed man, "please do it at a whisper." A brief pause. "Though, on second thought, that might be more disconcerting. Crazy people talking to themselves in whispers would be very unnerving indeed. Heaven knows what they'd be plotting."

"I'm not crazy," Harry said to him.

"Actually, Canberra is the capital of Australia," said the fat woman.

"I'm talking about your rat puppy, dammit!" said the voice inside Harry's head.

"Rat puppy?" Harry said. "What in the hell is a rat puppy?"

"Your Sydney Greenstreet, for Christ's sake! He's killing people, or had that slipped your mind?/You'd better start remembering, Harry, or you'll really fall behind."

"Sydney Greenstreet is killing people?" Harry asked. "He's only an actor. And, besides that, he's dead."

"So are you!"

"So am I what?"

"Dead, Fred. As dead as a snail who leaves no trail."

"Dead?" Harry was astonished. "That's the second time you've said that. I'm not dead!"

"As dead as last month's chicken cacciatore. Don't you recall,/The ocean, the fall . . . oh, shit!"

"Oh, shit? What's wrong?"

"I'm being plooped again."

"Plooped? What in the hell does 'plooped' mean?"

"You want to come with me, buddy?"

Harry hadn't noticed the cop standing in front of him.

"Sorry, my friend, you're on your own—"

"You listening to me, Mack?"

"Mack?" Harry focused on the cop. He was big, scowling and immovable. He took Harry by the arm and led him away.

Speaking to the Dead

Chapter Twenty-nine

Conrad was clearly happy to have people seated at his table. He decanted some Chablis, served it lovingly to everyone, explained that he had cheese and crackers besides and, if that wasn't enough, he could whip up a quick lunch of fettucine alfredo. But, inexplicably, no one was hungry anymore and only Morgan tried the wine, which he declared to be of an excellent vintage.

Conrad told them, "All that you see here—this house, the other buildings—is not the first . . . space that I've inhabited."

"Space?" Freely asked.

Conrad nodded. His rheumy gray eyes were friendly and intelligent. "It's the only word that really applies. I've been here . . . let me rephrase that, I've been *dead*, in the generally accepted meaning of the word, for ten years. At least, that's what I believe. As you might imagine, it is very difficult indeed to measure the passage of time in this place we have all inherited. There is no sun, as you know. And any 'days' and 'nights' we might have are, I would suspect, purely of our own creation. They may, in fact, well be subconscious creations, as is so much of what exists here, for us and *because* of us. We create . . . beings to populate our particular spaces, but these beings begin to act in ways we never anticipated. I believe it is because they are creations of our *whole* psyches. They aren't just creations of our conscious selves, our conscious wishes and desires, but of our *sub*conscious selves too. And as we all know, our subconscious selves are strangers to us."

He gestured to indicate the room. "I have my clocks, of course"—there were a dozen clocks in the room: two stately grandfather clocks, several mantel clocks, a cuckoo clock, a camelback clock and even three windup Big Bens in brass; all of them read 4:30 and all of them were ticking—"and my calendars, which you will see around the house. But still, days are almost impossible to keep track of. You look at the clock and it says . . . whatever it says, and you forget it. Then, when you look at the clock again and it says something else, you wonder how long it's been since you last looked at it. Sometimes you remember, sometimes you don't. Sometimes you think, Ah, that's the same time it was the last time I looked at it. And you decide that it has been twenty-four hours since you last looked at it, so you assume that a day has passed and you mark it on the calendar. But, of course, it might be only twelve hours that have passed. Half a day. But even this very rough approximation, this coincidence of clock watching, happens rarely. So it's extremely difficult to keep track of time. But with all of that said, I would estimate that

I have been dead for ten years." He smiled, as if an idea had just occurred to him. "Goodness, you can help me with that." He focused on Amelia. "What is the last date you remember? Month, day and year."

"Christmas Eve," she told him at once, and gave him the year.

His smile faded. "My God." He looked confusedly from face to face. "My God," he repeated, "if that's true, then I've been here for less than three years. It seems like so very much longer."

"You're talking about earth years," Morgan reminded him.

"There are no others," Conrad said.

Amelia said, "You're assuming that I haven't been here as long as you have. It's possible that I've been here longer."

Conrad thought about this and nodded. "Who knows? Maybe all my efforts at keeping track of time are stupid and futile. When we . . . passed over, didn't we leave all of that hogwash behind?"

Freely shrugged. "You grow accustomed to keeping track of things. Appointments, TV shows, gray hairs. Time. It's only human."

"And what are any of us if not 'only human,' eh?" Conrad asked.

Amelia changed the subject. "What is this place you've created for yourself here, Conrad?"

He frowned. "Mostly, what it is," he said. "What it has *become* for me is an cnigma. It has grown and changed since I created it. The beings I created have grown and changed as well, despite my best efforts to keep them precisely the way they were in the beginning."

"And how did you create them in the beginning?" Amelia asked.

"I suppose you could say that I created them to be . . . benevolent fiends," Conrad answered, with a twisted little smile.

Amelia shook her head. "I don't understand that."

His smile faded. He focused on the table, as if unwilling to look Amelia in the eye, and answered, "They were game pieces. No more, no less. That's the way I designed them and that's the way they acted. At first."

"You mean, like in chess?" Morgan asked. "They were like pawns and rooks and knights?"

"In a way, yes," Conrad answered. "They looked like human beings. Actually, I designed them to look like French partisans, from the Second World War. Eleven men, five women. Beautiful women, of course. I modeled them after a computer game I played while I was alive—"

"Really?" Morgan cut in. "What kind of computer did you have? A 386? A 486?"

"It was a 486, 33 megahertz, with 32 meg of ram and a CD-rom drive."

"I don't know what in the hell you're talking about," Amelia said. She glanced toward the door. She wished Jack would come inside. It made her unaccountably nervous to have him out there all by himself. Her maternal feelings surprised her.

Morgan was astonished. "Amelia, how can you live in the last decade of the twentieth century and not know a thing about computers?"

"Don't use my computer illiteracy to make a value judgment," Amelia replied testily. "As far as I'm concerned, the only thing that computers are good for is speeding up the pace of civilization, which is something it certainly doesn't need."

"Oh, c'mon," Morgan countered. "Computers have

allowed for all kinds of improvements . . . in medicine, armament, weather forecasting—"

"What we have," Amelia interrupted, "is a basic disagreement about what the direction of civilization should be—"

"Should have been," Conrad broke in. "Try to remember that we are all part of a very different sort of civilization now. And it's a civilization that may be far more anarchic than we realize."

"Anarchic?" Freely asked.

He nodded. "I think that once we left our physical selves behind, we entered a world of enormous and unpredictable possibility and potential. In the real world—in the world we left behind, I should say— our physical selves needed to work in harmony with the physical world in order to maintain our survival."

"Pardon me," Morgan said, "but I feel as *physical* as I ever did."

Conrad nodded. "There's an old saying that the most erogenous zone in the body is between our ears. I'm sure we all understand that. Our brains interpret and create our feelings and reactions, and our brains— our souls, really: I think that brains and souls are really one and the same thing—are telling us all now that we're as solid as we ever were. Hit the table"— he did it and got a loud thud for his effort—"and we expect a noise, and a little pain too, because that's something we grew accustomed to expect in our time on earth. So we expect it here, and our brains—our souls—happily oblige."

Freely said, "And what does all this have to do with your . . . benignly fiendish Frenchmen?" She smiled, pleased with her turn of phrase.

Conrad shrugged. "Nothing, probably. And maybe everything." He looked from face to face, then said to Amelia, "Tell me what you think this place is—heaven or hell?"

The question took her aback. She had never given it a thought. "I don't know." She shook her head. "It never occurred to me that it was either. I never really believed that there was actually a heaven or a hell."

This seemed to disappoint Conrad. He turned to Morgan. "And how about you? Heaven or hell?"

"Heaven. Of course." He paused. "At least, that's what I supposed at first. I'm not so sure now."

"We were always trained to believe in either a heaven or a hell, weren't we?" Freely asked.

"It's the old good or evil thing," Morgan said. "Either something is good or it's evil. No gray area. This place we've all become a part of may be a very, very large gray area."

"I think," Amelia offered, "that if these . . . creations of ours—your benevolent French fiends, Conrad and my Silver Lake weirdos—are what you say they are—combinations of both our conscious and unconscious selves—then we can learn a hell of a lot from them. About ourselves, I mean." She smiled. "Shit, maybe God created all of us so he could get in touch with *his* real self."

Conrad smiled back. "That whole idea may be part of the entire scheme of things here—"

Suddenly a shot rang out. Conrad jumped to his feet, shouting, "Good Lord, your friend is still in the car," and ran from the room. On the way, he scooped up what looked like a .45 automatic from a side-table drawer.

Amelia ran after him. Morgan and Freely followed.

Harry decided that he shouldn't tell these people about the voice he was hearing. Rat puppies, anarchists, Sydney Greenstreet, death. It had all the glaring earmarks of insanity.

But these people weren't paying him a lot of attention. They were eating donuts, drinking coffee, smoking. Most of them seemed to be attending to other matters, and the few that were concentrating on him—one of them a beefy detective wearing a soiled white shirt and what looked like a perpetual scowl—seemed to simply be trying to decide what to do with him. He heard the name "Bellevue" being bandied about, and he heard someone else say, "Oh, shit, let him go, he's not hurting anyone. So what if he's not wearing shoes?" And someone else grudgingly agreed.

Then a woman came over from another desk. She was tall, stocky, middle-aged, and had a no-nonsense look about her. She introduced herself as Mrs. Cantor and said she represented the Mental Health Crisis Intervention Committee, an arm of the New York County Social Services Department. "Mr. Briggs," she said—Harry didn't remember telling anyone his name, but supposed that he must have, otherwise she wouldn't know it—"would you say that you talk to people who aren't there often?"

Harry grinned at her. He was still wearing his brown trench coat and double-breasted gray suit, but his gun was missing—though not his shoulder holster. He didn't remember wearing a hat. "If you're asking whether I talk to myself a lot, the answer is no. I never talk to myself. I only talk aloud if other people are talking to me."

"Yes, quite," said Mrs. Cantor. "Perhaps my question was ill phrased. Let me try again."

"I wish you wouldn't," Harry said. "I understood it. And no, I don't talk to myself."

She nodded. "Mr. Briggs, who is the president of the United States?"

He told her.

She nodded again. "And what year is it?"

He told her the last year he remembered.

She smiled. "That is correct."

Harry cocked his head. "Of course it is."

"And how old are you, Mr. Briggs?"

"Forty-eight."

"And could you tell me why you're not wearing shoes?"

He leaned forward in the chair and looked at his bare feet. "I don't know," he answered. "I woke up in that building and my feet were bare—"

"You don't know what you were doing in that building, Mr. Briggs?"

"No."

"What *do* you remember?"

He sighed. "I remember my constitutional rights. And my constitutional rights say—"

"Forget it, Mack," said the beefy cop. "As far as we're concerned, you're just another crazy fucker. And crazy fuckers don't have no goddamned constitutional rights."

Mrs. Cantor glared at him. "Detective, if you don't mind, *I* am conducting this inquiry!"

"Am I being charged with something?" Harry asked.

"Not at this time," said Mrs. Cantor.

"*I'll* answer that," said the cop. He looked at Harry. "Whether you're being charged with something or not just ain't the point. We found you walking around barefoot in the snow, and talking to yourself, so we have to assume that you ain't got both oars in the water—"

"Oars in the water?" Harry interrupted. The phrase seemed to have some meaning for him, but he couldn't get hold of it.

"It's a slang term for mental or emotional distress," said Mrs. Cantor.

"I *know* what it means," Harry snapped.

"I'm back," he heard.

"Huh?" he said.

"Who are you talking to, Mr. Briggs?"

"I got plooped again,/It's really getting old,/I was back in sixth-grade English—"

"Plooped?" Harry interrupted.

"Mr. Briggs, *who* are you talking to?"

"I told you, sister, he's nuts. He's got toys in his attic."

"That will be all, Detective."

"Plooped, snooped, looped,/Just like you,/There's nothing I can do."

"I disagree," Harry said. "We all bear existential responsibility for ourselves and our actions."

"I say we ship the poor slob off to Bellevue!"

"Thankfully, Detective, you are not the one who makes those decisions."

"There was a young lady from Sparta—"

"Limericks?" Harry asked.

"Are limericks important to you, Mr. Briggs?" Mrs. Cantor asked.

He looked at her. Christ, he'd been talking to himself again. He shook his head. "No. Of course not."

"And what the hell is wrong with limericks?" the voice in Harry's head asked.

"Will you *shut* up!"

"He's losing it. Cuff him, Tony."

"You'll do no such thing. This man is clearly walking a very fine line—"

"He's walking a tightrope, lady, and he's going to fall straight into hell. Tony, cuff him!"

Chapter Thirty

Kennedy Whelan was bending over the broken body of a bellhop in a fifth-floor broom closet at the Ritz Carlton, and a man behind him was saying, "I saw who did this. He looked just like the guy in all those Humphrey Bogart movies."

Whelan glanced at the man speaking. He looked to be well into his eighties, and showed every day of it. "Peter Lorre?" Whelan asked.

The man shook his bald head earnestly. "No, no, no. Peter Lorre was short and thin. This man was large. Tall too. And he wore a . . . I got it! Sydney Greenstreet. The guy looked exactly like Sydney Greenstreet."

Whelan glanced at his partner. "Get the police artist down here."

Amelia, who was standing with Freely, Conrad and Morgan near the corner of one of the ugly, gray cinder-block buildings, nodded toward the monster Buick, which was not far away, and asked, "Are those some of the women you created?"

"Yes," Conrad answered sheepishly.

"Jesus, you must lead a hell of a fantasy life."

"I do," Conrad said. He was holding his .45 so it pointed up, near his temple. "At least, I did lead a hell of a fantasy life. It was very gratifying, at first—"

One of the women called out, "Hand yourself over to us, Conrad, or this man dies!" She and another of the voluptuous, scantily clad, dark-haired women were holding Jack South, who looked confused and very frightened. The woman who had called out was pointing what looked like a submachine gun at South's head.

Conrad called back, "Don't be afraid, young man. They're not going to do anything to you. I'm not absolutely sure they can."

"And not absolutely sure they can't either?" Morgan asked, grinning.

Jack South called, "If this is some kind of game—"

"It's not a game, monsieur. You tell him it is not a game, Conrad."

"No one believes it's a game anymore, Justine," Conrad called.

"Will *someone* give *someone* a straight answer!" Amelia fumed.

"There are no straight answers," Conrad told her.

"The fuck there aren't!" Amelia hissed, and stepped out into the open. "If you're going to shoot someone, shoot me!"

The French partisans looked confused. Justine called out, "Who is this woman taking your place, Conrad?"

"No one's taking my place!" he called back.

"Didn't you say there were men too?" Morgan asked.

"Yes," Conrad answered. "Eleven men. The women killed them."

"You're kidding."

"No. They're strong women. I've always liked strong women." He paused meaningfully. "But I'm afraid that these women turned out to be quite a bit stronger than I'd bargained for."

"And what do they want with you?"

"God only knows."

Morgan smiled. "And as far as they're concerned, that's you."

"Me."

"Sure. To them, you're God."

"Oh. Of course," Conrad said, as if the concept were wearyingly familiar to him.

Amelia took a couple of steps toward the monster Buick. "Let him go, bitch!"

"I am no *bitch!* I am Justine, reluctant but fearless fighter for the causes of justice and independence and a free France!"

Amelia laughed.

"Don't laugh at her," Conrad warned. "They don't like to be laughed at."

Amelia took another couple of steps toward the Buick. The scantily clad French partisans continued to look confused.

Morgan said, "Maybe they don't like *you* to laugh at them."

Conrad grimaced, as if he knew that this was also the truth.

"Let the man *go!*" Amelia commanded.

And the French partisans turned and ran, weapons held high, breasts and fannies moving deliciously.

Amelia glanced at Conrad. His intelligent, rheumy gray eyes were lit up with lust. "Christ," she whispered. "No wonder they're trying to get hold of you. You've made them slaves to your fucking libido. What woman wants that?"

Conrad was amazed. "What are you talking about? They're *my* creations, after all!"

"Are they?" Amelia asked. "Are they really?" Then she went to Jack South, who was trembling, and put him in the front passenger seat of the car. She called to Morgan and Freely, who came at once.

"You believe I'm a devil, don't you?" said Conrad.

"No. None of us is a devil. I don't believe in devils."

He nodded. "I understand that."

Amelia said, "My people need spaces of their own. How do I find them?"

Conrad shook his head dismally. "I don't really know. I imagine you simply . . . look. How did you find your space?"

Amelia thought about this. She wasn't sure. It was simply *there* for her.

Conrad continued, "There are probably billions of spaces, but finding them, and melding with them, is in all likelihood a very time-consuming thing. I wish you luck."

"Sure," Amelia said drily, rolling up her window, and, without another word, drove off.

Within moments, Conrad and his ugly gray buildings were behind them and they were once again in the midst of the waving sunflowers and blue-green sky.

"That's him!" declared the bald octogenarian to the police artist. "That's the man. Sydney Greenstreet!"

The artist looked at the drawing that he'd created under the old man's guidance. He was not a connoisseur of detective films, but he knew that the face staring back at him from the sketch pad was indeed the face of Sydney Greenstreet.

"Jesus," he said, "you're right."

"Of course I'm right, young man," the old man told him. "He's the one who killed that poor bellhop, and you can take that straight to the bank!"

"Yes," said the artist, "I think I will."

"Address?" the detective asked Harry.

"Chappaqua," Harry answered.

"Where in Chappaqua?"

"Portland Road. Number Twenty-six." Harry felt a sudden discomfort, as if something were pulling on him everywhere at once. He frowned.

The detective gave him an incredulous look. "You're telling me that you live on Portland Road in Chappaqua and yet you're running around barefoot and in that getup?" He nodded to indicate Harry's soiled brown trench coat and double-breasted gray suit.

Harry looked at himself. "What's wrong with this getup?"

The detective sighed. "Phone number?"

Harry tried to remember his phone number. He couldn't. "I can't remember," he said.

"No problem. We'll get it," the detective said, and pulled a thick phone book out of one of his desk drawers. A moment later, he wrote a number down on Harry's booking sheet.

Harry said, "Do I really need to wear these handcuffs?" They were chafing him.

The detective glanced at him, then back at the

booking sheet. "Yes, you do," he said tersely.

"Because I talk to myself and I don't wear shoes?"

"That's right," the detective answered, and smiled quickly. "We have to determine that you're not a danger to yourself or to others."

"I can tell you that. Just ask me."

"Sure," the cop said, and smiled again. He picked up the phone, dialed a number, waited, then hung up the phone. "You married, Mr. Briggs?"

"Yes."

"How come no one answers the phone at your house?"

"I don't know." He shook his head. Why *didn't* Barbara answer, indeed?

"I'll try again," the detective said. "Maybe I dialed wrong the first time."

Sydney, who was seated in a big wingback chair in his hotel room at the Ritz Carlton, was contented. Life was good. Death was good. He felt sated, if only temporarily. A full stomach and a quieted libido. What more could a man need?

Sleep, perhaps?

Sleep? Close the eyes, lapse into unconsciousness and leave oneself as vulnerable as an infant. Where had that dreadful idea come from? Didn't one need to be *tired* in order to sleep?

He stood, went to the door, tested the knob to be sure it was locked and then slid the bolt across too.

It was possible that he *was* tired, now that he thought about it.

He went to the bed and regarded it with uncertainty. Perhaps *this* was the tug he'd been feeling. Sleepiness. He had seen others sleep—Anna Freely, for instance—but had never felt the need for it himself, until now.

He took off his black suit jacket, hung it neatly in the closet, returned to the bed, patted it with one meaty hand and lay down on his back. What were these changes taking place within him? he wondered.

Unconsciousness came almost at once.

"Do you mind if I turn on the radio?" Jack South asked. "I need music." He was still trembling.

"Sure, go ahead," Amelia said.

The road had narrowed considerably, had become very badly rutted, and Amelia wasn't sure the Buick's suspension was up to the test.

Jack turned the dials. Music blared out at once—Hank Williams, which Jack declared to be unlistenable, although, amazingly, Morgan objected from the backseat that country music was "the most listenable music ever produced." Jack turned to another station. Karen Carpenter's voice filled the car.

Amelia squirmed and grimaced. "Please," she said, "something else."

"I like it," Freely said.

"Yeah, well *I* don't," Jack said, "and I got control of the radio." He turned to another station. News, apparently. He prepared to change channels again, but Amelia reached out and stayed his hand.

"No," she said.

He shrugged. "Okay. You're the boss."

". . . additional mapping will be attempted soon, according to Mr. Fuller, who also reported vague magnetic shifts at various points," the announcer was saying. "Such shifts have also been reported by airplane pilots flying within their own spaces. Mr. Fuller also tells us that an attempt at high-altitude exploration has again been made by Rosalind Moore, whose last attempt ended in failure. This time, says Mr. Fuller, Ms. Moore's high-altitude explorations yielded some very interesting data."

Silence. Then John Lennon's "Instant Karma" came on.

"Hey!" Freely shouted from the backseat. "I was listening to that. It was interesting."

Jack South gave her an exasperated look. "I didn't touch it," he said.

"You know what it sounded like?" Morgan said. "It sounded like someone is trying to map out this place we're in. It sounded like this place has its own kinds of geographers and explorers."

"And it also sounded like they've been pretty unsuccessful so far," Amelia said.

"Do you believe she's at home?" the detective asked Harry.

"Tell him to fuck off," said the voice in Harry's head. "What can he do to you?"

Harry ignored the voice. He had begun to think of it as an annoyance, and ever since then the voice had grown weaker and less insistent. Harry said, "I'm sure Barbara's home."

"Is she hard of hearing?"

"No."

"Do you think I should call the police in Chappaqua and have them check it out? It's possible that your wife's in some kind of trouble."

Harry shrugged. "You'll have the house checked out whether I think you should or not."

The detective grinned. "Smart boy." He picked up the phone and dialed a number. "Yeah, this is Detective Gribbons, Manhattan North. I was wondering if you could do me a little favor."

On Portland Road, in Chappaqua, two boys in their midteens had stopped their snowmobiles at the top of a rise that overlooked a sparsely populated area of upscale homes, neat gardens and heated swimming pools. The snowmobiles were Christmas presents—presented a day early—and the boys were not yet completely comfortable with them, although they drove them over the pasture country that belonged to their "Gentleman Farmer" fathers as if they were immortal.

One of the boys nodded toward a house not far off and said, "Hey, look at that."

The other boy looked. "What is it?" he asked, because his glasses were beginning to fog now that the snowmobiles had stopped.

"It looks like a naked lady," the first boy said.

The other boy wiped off his glasses and looked again. "Yeah," he said. "A naked lady floating in the water."

Chapter Thirty-one

Kennedy Whelan was on his way to Manhattan North to see a policewoman who was stationed there. She was tall, substantial, attractive, bright and strong.

Whelan had decided to give sex one more chance. He'd convinced himself that sex was the only real reason that men and women got together. Otherwise, men would simply get together with men and women would get together with women. He'd convinced himself of this absurdity because his last fling had been with a woman who had thrown him over for a younger man and it had lacerated his ego. The policewoman at Manhattan North, he told himself, looked as though she'd be a tiger in the sack. Wide hips, double-X tits. She'd ride him, screaming out her pleasure, until next Tuesday.

When Whelan thought like this, he blushed. He was alone in the car, so there was no one to see him, but he looked around anyway. The people walking the early evening, snow-covered streets of Manhattan paid him no attention.

Amelia brought the monster Buick to a jarring stop. The rutted road had ended. There were no more fields of grass and sunflowers, and no more blue-green sky. Instead, the sky was gray and in turmoil, as if immense, ghostly armies battled within it. The landscape was barren, windswept and dotted with emaciated trees and clumps of spiky, dark grasses.

Amelia whispered, "What the hell is this?"

"I think *hell* is exactly the right word," Morgan said.

Jack South said, "It's neat. I like it."

"You would," Morgan retorted.

"I'm all for turning around and going back the way we came," Freely added.

"Well, we certainly can't go forward, can we?" Amelia pointed out. She was right. There was no road.

"We could walk," Jack South suggested.

A scream broke through the white noise of the air-conditioning and the car radio—Ricky Nelson belting out "I'm a traveling man, made a lot of stops . . ."

"Jesus, did you hear that?" Morgan whispered. "Someone screamed."

"Yes," Amelia said, and turned off the radio. "I heard it too."

Another scream, which seemed louder, because the radio was now silent.

"Someone's in trouble out there," Morgan said.

Amelia didn't reply.

Freely said, "I really don't like this. If you're not going to turn around, I'm going to walk."

Amelia looked back at her. "I'm not sure how far

you'd get," she said. "I think that in order to survive, we have to keep moving."

"You could be wrong," Morgan said.

Amelia nodded. "I could be. Yes."

"And it wouldn't be the first time," Freely pointed out.

Amelia sighed. "Yes, I'm aware of that. I'm as human and as fallible as anyone."

Jack South opened his door and stepped out onto the bleak, windswept landscape. He got back in at once and shut the door hard. "It smells bad."

"Oh, like what?" Morgan asked.

"I don't know. Rotten eggs."

Freely chuckled. "Sulfur. It fits."

"And there ain't no wind," Jack added. "It only looks like there's wind." This seemed to disappoint him.

There was another scream, closer this time. Amelia saw movement ahead, at the crest of a little hillock dotted with stunted, nasty-looking clumps of dark grasses. "What's that?" she said. She could see very little—the top of a blond head, a narrow expanse of white skin.

"I say we vamoose!" Morgan said.

"I second that," Freely added.

Amelia nodded briskly, put the car in reverse and tromped on the accelerator. Nothing. She looked at the dashboard. All the red warning lights were lit. The engine was off. "Shit!" she whispered, put the car in park again and turned on the engine. It fired up at once, but then shut off. "Shit!" she repeated.

"Don't flood it!" Morgan warned.

"I'm not flooding it!" Amelia shot back. "I know how to drive, goddammit!" She turned the engine back on and pushed the accelerator halfway to the floor, thinking the idle might be too low.

"You're going to flood it!" Morgan shouted.

Amelia put the car in reverse again. It screamed backward. The blue-green sky and nodding sunflowers reappeared. She smiled. Success.

The engine shut off. "Dammit to hell!" she cried, and looked at the gas gauge. It read empty. "Great," she whispered. Wasn't this a fine kettle of fish? Where in the hell was she going to find gas around *here?*

"What's wrong?" Freely asked, and leaned forward, so her face was close to Amelia's neck. "Oh," she said dismally, "out of gas. That's too bad."

"Yes, it is," Amelia said. "And it appears that we have no choice now but to walk."

She was looking at Freely as she said this. Morgan was sitting next to her. Suddenly his jaw dropped and his eyes opened wide. Amelia turned and saw through the windshield just what he was seeing. As if it were expanding from within, the bleak, windswept landscape and gray sky in turmoil had overtaken them. She turned her head quickly, looked through the rear window, saw the hint of sunflowers, green grasses and blue-green sky. Then it was gone.

Everyone stayed quiet for a long moment.

Then Morgan whispered, "It's some kind of trap. It feels like a trap."

Amelia tried the engine again.

"Don't do that," Morgan shouted, and leaned forward, so his torso was over the back of the front seat. "You'll wear down the battery."

"Leave her alone!" Jack South warned.

Morgan looked quickly at him, grinned a little, then sat back. "I'm staying put," he said. "Whatever it is that's brought us here—"

"*We've* brought us here," Amelia told him.

"It doesn't matter," Morgan declared. "We're here and whoever is responsible for this . . . nightmare is probably only too happy to have us wandering about unprotected."

"You don't *know* that!" Jack shouted at him.

"It's okay," Amelia said. "He's probably right. I think we have to assume that he's right at any rate."

"So we're just going to sit here?" Freely asked, astonished.

"I really don't think there's anything else we can do," Amelia answered.

Jack turned on the radio.

"Not right now," Amelia said, and reached to turn it off. There was a loud burst of static and she jerked her hand back, as if the radio were going to bite her.

Jack tried the tuning knob. Nothing. "Dammit! No music."

Amelia turned the radio off.

"It's getting cold in here," Morgan said.

He was right. The temperature had dropped a good ten degrees in the last few minutes. Amelia opened her door. The air outside was cold, dank, forbidding.

"We've really stepped in it this time," Freely said.

"I told you," Morgan said. "It's a trap."

They heard another scream, closer. Desperately, Amelia tried the ignition again, but with no luck.

"What's that?" Jack said, and pointed out of the driver's window.

All of them looked. They saw what appeared to be a huge, dark house at the horizon.

Freely shivered. "It's creepy," she said.

"It's some asshole's idea of a haunted house, that's what it is!" Morgan said. "And I think we'd better just stay away from it."

The car was getting colder. Goose bumps rose on Amelia's arm. "I don't think we have a choice," she said. "I think if we stay here, we'll freeze."

"To death?" Jack said, and laughed falscly.

"That's enough," Amelia scolded.

Jack stopped laughing.

"It's probably better to freeze to death than to freeze forever," Morgan said drily. "But I think if we try to hike across this landscape, we'll freeze anyway. That house is a couple of miles away. I mean, look at you, Amelia." She was dressed in her white shorts and white shirt.

"Again," she said, "I doubt that we have a choice. I think we're being *coaxed*. And I think that if whoever's coaxing us wanted to harm us, he'd have done it by now. I think it's another game and I think we have to play along." She opened her door, stepped out and started walking.

Jack followed at once and caught up with her, sniffling because of the pervasive smell of sulfur that hung in the air like a fog. After a few moments, Morgan and Freely got out of the car too and fell in behind. And as the little group walked toward the huge, dark house at the horizon, the air grew steadily warmer and clearer, and Amelia thought, Yes, we *are* being coaxed.

But why? she wondered. And by whom?

The boy on the snowmobile nudged his companion and told him, "She's dead. I think she's dead," meaning the naked woman floating facedown in the heated pool.

The other boy didn't know what to say. He could tell his friend was right about the woman, but all he could do was stare at her.

"I think we gotta do something," said the first boy.

A man appeared at the edge of the pool. He stood looking at the woman for a minute, jumped in, thrashed about for a while and then quieted.

"Holy shit!" whispered the first boy.

"We gotta do something," said the second boy, happy to have his voice back at last.

"Yeah, I know. I said that. But what do we do?"

"We go back home and call someone."

"Maybe we should try and help those people first."

"Help them what? They're drowned. What are we going to help them with?"

"I don't know. Maybe they're not drowned. Maybe they're still alive." He revved up his snowmobile, as if getting ready to take off.

The other boy shook his head. "Naw, they're drowned. Can't you tell? Look at 'em."

They both looked for several minutes and then the first boy said, "Well, if they weren't drowned before, they sure are now."

"Sorry, Mr. Briggs," said the cop, as he ushered Harry into a holding cell, "I know it's a lousy way to have to spend your Christmas Eve."

"Christmas Eve?" Harry said.

The cop locked the cell door. "Don't tell me you don't know what day it is?"

Harry shook his head.

The cop tutted pityingly and nodded at Harry's bare feet. "I think I can find some shoes that'll fit you, Mr. Briggs. What size do you wear? I'd guess eleven."

Harry looked at his feet a moment, then at the cop. "It can't be Christmas Eve! What the hell am I doing here on Christmas Eve? I should be home with my wife."

"Yeah," said the cop, "me too. But I'm stuck here. I'm afraid we're both stuck here." He looked at Harry's feet again. "Size eleven. That sounds about right to me," he said, and walked off.

"The world's full of assholes," Harry heard. "But don't pin *him* down/Because he won't stop squirming,/He'll just thrash around." It was the voice in his head again and Harry wasn't sure if he welcomed it.

The voice went on, "Meaning that he's right as rain, Harry,/Remember me—your friend in pain,/No, no, you're not insane. It's really me,/And if you can't see,/There must be a key,/A reason for the season."

Harry nodded glumly. "Yes," he whispered. "I remember you. You're my sanity tiptoeing off into Never-Never Land."

The voice chuckled.

Harry grimaced. His inner voice was not only rhyming at him again, it was laughing at him too. That certainly wasn't a good sign.

The voice said, "You made your little ride to the other side/And here you are/And here am I—"

"Stop!" Harry shouted.

"Stop?" the voice said.

"Yes, that's very aggravating."

"What's aggravating?"

"That damned rhyming."

"Oh," the voice said, sounding cowed. "Habit. I get loose on my own over here and that's what I do. I rhyme."

"Just please don't do it anymore, okay?"

"Okay."

"Thanks."

"Do you know, Harry, that you made a little hippity-hop back in time? Don't ask me how. Or why. Maybe we have to go back to the moment that we

239

T. M. Wright

died. Or earlier. Maybe if the world goes on without us . . ." The voice faltered.

"Yes?" Harry said. "Go on."

"I'd like to, but I can't. What do I know really? I'm just a passenger on this train."

"Aren't we all?" Harry whispered.

"But I'll tell you what I *do* know. I think. You're alive again. Alive, alive-o. Breathing and sweating and salivating, and for real. Enjoy it while you can, my space-hopping friend, because I think your good fortune will come to an end."

"Marvelous," Harry whispered.

"Interesting anyway," said the voice.

Harry sighed.

"You're confused, aren't you?" the voice asked.

"Yes, I am," Harry answered.

"You think *I'm* . . . not real. Is that right?"

Harry said nothing.

"I thought so," said the voice, and sighed. "This is going to be tough."

The cop reappeared. He had a pair of black oxfords in his hand. "Try these on, Mr. Briggs," he said, and pushed the shoes through the bars.

Harry stared at the shoes for a moment, uncomprehendingly.

"Go ahead," said the cop, "try them on. I can't give you the laces. Sorry."

"Sam Goodlow," said the voice in Harry's head. "Remember me?"

"Sam Goodlow?" Harry whispered.

"Sorry?" said the cop.

Harry looked at him. "Sam Goodlow?" he repeated.

The cop shook his head. "No. Robert Lawrence."

"Shit!" said the voice in Harry's head. "Okay, how about Sydney Greenstreet?"

240

"Sydney Greenstreet?" Harry said aloud. It had the ring of familiarity to it.

"No, Robert Lawrence," the cop repeated. "Not Sydney Greenstreet. Maybe you oughta get some shut-eye, Mr. Briggs."

The voice in Harry's head said, "We came here to find him and bring him back to Silver Lake./For pity's sake,/This is no cake ... walk you're on, my time-hopping friend,/Your rat puppy is bringing people's lives to an end."

"I told you to stop rhyming at me, dammit!" Harry shouted.

"Rhyming?" said the cop.

"Sydney Greenstreet," said the voice in Harry's head.

"Sydney Greenstreet?" Harry whispered. The name was so hauntingly familiar.

"Just try to get some sleep," the cop said. "I'd guess you have a long day ahead of you tomorrow."

Kennedy Whelan walked past the desk sergeant at Manhattan North and said, "Sure, merry Christmas to you too," and then went into the squad room to find the policewoman who had put his libido in a stranglehold. He stopped just inside the entrance to the big room and looked around. It was nearly empty. A beefy detective he didn't recognize sat at the far desk, eating a jelly donut and poring over a copy of the *Daily News*, and close by a young, bearded cop with a ponytail looked up from some plastic bags filled with what looked like heroin, smiled and said, "Ho-ho-ho, Ken."

Whelan said, "Yeah, ho-ho," and asked if the policewoman was out.

The cop nodded. "Home with her husband."

"Husband?" She'd never mentioned a husband.

"Yeah. She's been married ten years." He cocked his head. "She never told you that, Ken?"

Whelan shrugged. "Sure, she told me."

"Sorry," the young cop said.

"Me too," Whelan said, fished a cigar from his pocket and lit it. To hell with trying to quit.

Two uniformed cops passed by on their way into the squad room. One of them said to the other, "I told him, 'No, my name ain't Sydney Greenstreet, it's Robert Lawrence.' The guy's nuttier than a fruitcake, poor slob."

Whelan called after them, "Hold on a moment."

The Reunion

Chapter Thirty-two

The huge, dark house that Amelia, Jack, Morgan and Freely approached sat precariously at the edge of a high, rocky cliff overlooking a dark and choppy sea. This sea appeared to rise at the gray and tumultuous horizon, as if it were preparing to overtake the land and sweep them all away. At first, this illusion was very disconcerting, but as the group moved closer to the house, the sea didn't grow, or change, and everyone in the group accepted that it was merely a bizarre facet of this space, the design of a madman.

As they drew to within a couple of hundred yards of the house, Freely said, "It looks like something out of a Gothic romance."

"It's creepy as a bug," Morgan said, which the others were surprised to hear from him.

There were several dozen long, narrow, multipaned windows at the front of the house. The house itself bore three gables and a steeply sloping slate roof that

245

boasted four tall, grotesquely ornate chimneys.

Huge, obscenely grinning, wild-eyed cherubs carrying dark pink gargoyles in their teeth peered down from several of the roof edges.

One light burned in a third-story window, but as the group approached over the barren landscape, this light went out.

"It's a bit stereotypical," Freely said.

"Stereotypical?" Jack South asked.

"Sure. It's like part of a Halloween pop-up book or something. It goes beyond spooky and into the ridiculous."

"Speak for yourself," Morgan said.

"Yeah," Jack agreed. "Speak for yourself."

"The guy who created this has almost no imagination at all," Freely said. "Except for those nasty cherubs." She stopped walking and looked up at them. "I mean, they *are* a pretty nifty touch. Not simply sinister gargoyles and a host of irritatingly saccharine cherubs, but nasty cherubs with baby gargoyles in their teeth." She smiled. "I like it."

Amelia reached back and grabbed her arm. "C'mon," she said, "we're almost there," and they were.

Harry—head in hands and eyes closed—was sitting on the hardboard cot that served as a bed in the holding cell, trying to ignore the increasingly insistent voice in his head—"You're dead, goddammit! Don't you remember? The little rowboat. The ocean. The bulbous thing with the wild eyes . . ."—when Kennedy Whelan startled him by saying, from outside the holding cell, "What do you know about Sydney Greenstreet?"

246

He lurched, looked wide-eyed at Whelan and said, "Huh? Sydney Greenstreet?"

"Yeah. What do you know about him?"

"Nothing. I know he's an actor."

"What else?"

The voice in Harry's head said, "Don't mess with this guy. He means business."

"What *should* I know?" Harry asked.

Whelan grinned. Progress.

The words etched in Gothic script in stone above the huge, arched doorway read: ABANDON HOPE, ALL YE WHO ENTER HERE.

"Charming," said Freely.

She looked closer. There were other words etched beneath, but they were very small, and done less expertly, so they were harder to make out. "Can you read that?" she asked Morgan.

He looked. "Yeah, I think so."

Amelia read, " 'Mothers and Fathers welcome.' "

Jack South chuckled. "Someone thinks he's funny."

Amelia stepped forward and looked for a door knocker. She saw none.

"Look there," Morgan said, pointing to the right of the door. "I think it's a doorbell."

Amelia looked. "A doorbell?" she said incredulously. She rang it.

Loud, basso-profundo thudding, as if from a huge door knocker, arose within the house.

Amelia grimaced, while Jack South smiled uneasily.

"Now *that's* a doorbell!" Morgan declared.

"This guy's okay," Freely said.

"I don't know—something feels . . . wrong here," Amelia said.

"That's the understatement of the millennium," Morgan said.

"I mean," Amelia explained, "these little creative touches are very . . . interesting, sure. But there's something . . . wrong here," she repeated, "and I can't pinpoint it."

"I think you're being female," Morgan told her.

She ignored him. No one had answered the door, so she rang the doorbell again.

Jack South asked, "Did you notice how clear the air is? That rotten egg smell is gone."

"Yes," Amelia replied. "It disappeared as we got closer to the house. Someone's drawing us in."

"That's what I think," Freely agreed. "Someone's drawing us in."

"It's a trap," Morgan said.

"And if it is," Amelia pointed out, "there's absolutely nothing we can do about it."

Suddenly, the huge door opened.

A plainclothes cop came into the holding area and said, "Mr. Briggs, you're going to have to come with me."

"Wait a minute," Whelan snapped. "I'm questioning this man."

"Sorry. This is urgent."

"What's going on?" Harry asked, and stood.

"You live at Twenty-six Portland Road, in Chappaqua?" the plainclothes cop asked. "Is that correct?"

"Yes, it is. But I don't understand—"

The cop unlocked the cell door and ordered Harry to turn around and put his hands behind his back, which Harry did.

The cop glanced at Whelan, said, "Watch him, would you?" and went into Harry's cell.

"For Christ's sake," Whelan said, "this man may be a key witness to a string of murders—"

"Later," the cop said, handcuffing Harry and leading him from the holding area, out of the precinct house. He put him into the backseat of a waiting squad car and got in beside him.

"Where are you taking me?" Harry asked.

"Home," the cop answered. "Okay, driver, let's go."

Sydney dreamed about cold water, gray snow, dirty hands, ducks with their beaks sawn off, black earth. He smiled as he dreamed. Saliva pooled at the edge of his mouth. His small eyes moved rapidly beneath their white lids. His little cock stirred and rose up.

The dream evaporated. His erection evaporated.

He felt himself being tugged again, on all sides, as if something *under* his skin were pushing outward on every square inch of his substantial body.

He thought that he was coming apart, and he woke up screaming.

Amelia, Morgan, Jack and Freely had to squint against the light that flooded over them from within the house. It took minutes for their eyes to adjust to it, and when they did, none of them understood what they were seeing.

Tilt-a-whirls tilted and whirled.

Popcorn machines belched popcorn.

Trampolines springed and sproinged, though they were empty.

Multicolored plastic balls inside big mesh cages rolled endlessly.

And there were swings and slides and teeter-totters. Jungle gyms too. And puppet theaters.

Then they saw a little boy of eight or nine at the far end of the gigantic room. He was dressed in blue shorts and a red and white polo shirt, and he sat on a huge, ornate, pink chair.

Amelia started across the room toward him.

He looked up at her suddenly. "You'd better go away!" he shouted.

"Why?" Amelia shouted back. The noise from all the paraphernalia in the room was deafening.

The boy looked at her confusedly.

"Why should we go away?" Amelia shouted again. "We have noplace to go."

The boy rose from his chair. He was short—even for his apparent age—and he was wiry and intelligent looking. "Did you bring my Mom and Dad with you?"

Amelia shook her head. "I'm sorry, no. Are they outside?"

The boy nodded, smiling. "They've been out there a long, long time. A hundred years, I think."

"And you're in here all alone?"

He nodded vigorously. "Except for you now." This seemed to please him.

It did not please Amelia. The boy made her uneasy, though she couldn't figure out why. Perhaps he didn't seem completely *real*, though she rejected this idea at once. He was at least as real as they were. Obvious, as well, that he had to be very unhappy in this big house all by himself.

"What is this place?" Amelia asked.

The boy smiled oddly. "I call it 'The Octopus.' "

Amelia was having trouble hearing him over the din. She took a couple of steps forward, then stopped. The boy was still fifty feet away. "That's an interesting name for a house. Why do you call it that?"

250

"Because it reaches out like an octopus does."

"Reaches out?" She was growing apprehensive.

He nodded earnestly. "Like an octopus," he repeated. "You think you're far enough from it and it's not going to get you, but you aren't. It reaches out."

She remembered the way the dark sky in turmoil had seemed to follow them, even though she'd backed away from it, into the blue-green sky and nodding sunflowers.

"Is that what happened to your parents?" she asked.

He nodded. "Uh-huh."

"But you got away from it?"

He smiled oddly again, but said nothing.

"Isn't that what happened?" Amelia asked again.

"He's a creepy little kid," Morgan said, behind her.

"I don't think he's a kid at all," Jack South suggested.

"Tell them to shut up!" the boy demanded.

Amelia took a couple more steps forward, stopped, cocked her head. She could see the boy more clearly now and his paper-white face had an odd look to it, as if his skin were marbled.

"Could you tell me your name?" she asked.

"Tell me yours first."

"Amelia," she said, then glanced at the rest of the group. "And these are my friends—Jack, Morgan and Freely."

"Do you know why I'm here, Amelia?" the boy asked.

"Perhaps you could tell me *your* name first." She took another couple of steps forward.

The boy said, "My name is Billy, George, Jimmy, Stephen, John."

"That's a lot of names."

"And I *made* this house, and all the stuff outside too."

"That was very creative of you."

"This stuff inside is all shitty stuff." He moved his hand to indicate the tilt-a-whirls, the trampolines, the swings and teeter-totters. "Who wants this stuff?"

"You don't want it, Billy, George, Jimmy . . ."

"My mom and dad made it for me. They wanted a little boy, so they made me. And they wanted a place for me to play, so they made *this*. But it wasn't what *I* wanted and they knew it. They didn't care. It didn't matter what I wanted. I wasn't really real. Who cares what little boys who aren't really real want!"

"You're not real, Jimmy, George, Billy . . ."

"*You're* real," he interrupted. "I can tell. You ask questions all the time. That's what real people do. They ask lots of questions. Like my mom and dad did. 'Why did you make our house look like this? It's awful. Why don't you like the toys we make for you?' Stupid questions. But they're paying for what they tried to do to me, and someday all this stuff will be gone, and they'll be gone too. And I'll be really alone." Another odd smile. Broader. More malicious.

"Is that what you want, Billy, George, John?" Amelia asked. "To be alone?"

He stepped forward, stopped, stepped forward again, stopped. His movements were very stiff, as if he were a windup toy. And as he got closer, Amelia could see that the marbling effect she'd noticed before was real—his skin looked as if it were made of cracked porcelain. "Real people don't want to be alone," he said, smirking. "That's why my mom and dad made me. Because they were all alone."

"I say we take our chances outside," Morgan shouted.

Amelia glanced around at him. He was beginning to turn toward the door. "No," she said. "We can't go back out there. There's noplace for us to go."

"And noplace for us to stay either," Freely said.

"She's right!" agreed Jack South.

The boy was grinning. His small, dark eyes were like marbles. Suddenly Amelia knew that they couldn't stay here, with this creature.

She turned quickly spread her arms to encompass the group behind her and, en masse, they made their way to the door.

Chapter Thirty-three

The detective unzipped the body bag before it was loaded into the medical examiner's station wagon and said, "Mr. Briggs, is this your wife?"

Harry stared at the woman's face for a long while. At last, he said firmly, "My wife's not dead. She's alive. She's as alive as you or I."

"Could you simply tell me if this is your wife, Mr. Briggs?"

Harry nodded. "Yes, that's Barbara. But she's not dead."

"So, it's all coming back to you, huh, Harry?" said the voice in his head.

The cop unzipped another bag, lying beside Barbara's body, near the heated swimming pool. "And who is this, Mr. Briggs?"

Harry looked. "I know him," he said. "His name was Harry Briggs."

The cop sighed. "That's *your* name, sir."

"Yes, and that *was* me, there, under the sheet. I have to tell you that it's very, very disconcerting to see myself that way."

The cop shook his head in frustration. "This man is your brother, right? He's your twin?"

"No, that's not what I said. I said he's *me*. He has a birthmark on the inside of his right thigh. I do too."

"Mr. Briggs, I can understand that . . . all of this might be a shock for you—"

"Do you know where I come from, Detective?" Harry felt suddenly uncomfortable. His arms tingled. His legs too. And his feet, his hands.

The detective stared bemusedly at him for a moment, then said simply, "No. Tell me."

Harry glanced confusedly at his feet, then, with conviction, at the detective. "I come from the other side. And do you know why I'm here?"

"When you say 'the other side,' Mr. Briggs, what exactly do you . . ."

Harry couldn't feel his hands and feet anymore. He looked at his feet again. He lifted his right foot, looked at his heel. He thought he knew what was happening. He said, "I mean heaven, or maybe hell, the afterlife, whatever you wish to call it. That's where I've come from. It should be obvious. That's me there, under the sheet. And that's my wife. That's my temporal body at any rate, and that's my wife's temporal body—"

"Jerry," the detective interrupted, addressing a uniformed cop nearby, "would you please take Mr. Briggs back to the precinct house and call Bellevue—"

Harry, still handcuffed, did a zigzag around the two cops and dove headfirst into the pool.

* * *

"If anything's scary about all this," Amelia said, as the huge door to the big, dark house closed behind them, "*that*'s scary."

"What?" Jack South asked.

"The fact that our creations themselves can create—" Amelia began.

"I'll tell you what scares me," Freely cut in. "I can't see the car, I can't see blue sky." A ragged scream erupted from somewhere beyond them. "*That* scares me!"

"Amelia, I don't understand," Morgan said. "What creations are you talking about?"

"The people of Silver Lake, for instance," she answered. "They're my creations. They're not real people. They're projections."

Another ragged scream rose up from the bleak, windswept landscape.

"Jesus!" Jack South whispered.

Amelia continued, "I wanted a little community filled with pleasant but quirky people, so I created Silver Lake. And I populated it with people like Leonard and Mrs. Alexander and Mrs. Conte and Viola Pennypacker, poor woman—"

"And this boy is one of those people?" Morgan asked.

"He's not one of *mine*," Amelia answered tersely. "He's obviously something his 'parents' conjured up."

Another scream. "And I'd guess," Freely said, "that that's one of his parents now!"

Amelia nodded. "And they conjured up all those . . . things inside the house too, so their 'little boy' could amuse himself. But when they conjured him up, they didn't realize what a lot of us don't realize—that our creations are not simply products of our conscious selves, they're products of our *whole* selves, and obviously there was something about them, this boy's parents, that . . ."

"And he doesn't like what they made for him?" Freely asked. "The swings and teeter-totters."

"Obviously not," Amelia answered. "These people created a creature of darkness."

"And what do you think that creature wants with us?" Morgan asked.

"Heaven knows," Amelia answered.

"Then there's no one in *this* place who can tell us a thing," Morgan quipped.

"I ain't staying here," Jack South announced, and began walking away from the house.

"Jack," Amelia called after him, "I don't think we should go anywhere without talking about it first—"

"Then go ahead and talk," he called back. "Talk all you want. I'm sick of talking." He walked faster.

Amelia ran after him, caught him up and grabbed his arm. He carried on walking and she kept pace with him, hand on his arm. "Jack, please, I believe we should all put our heads together about this—"

"Yeah," he cut in, smiling grimly, "and create a four-headed monster!"

Amelia glanced back at Morgan and Freely, who were still standing in front of the door to the dark house. They looked very worried. "Listen, Jack," she said, "if we go much farther, we're going to lose track of our friends. Why don't we just turn around—"

"I'm not a child!" he snapped.

This surprised Amelia. "I didn't realize I was treating you like one."

"Well, you are. And you were. And I don't like it."

"Jack, I'm sorry, I . . ." She realized that what he was saying was true.

"Just don't do it anymore, okay?"

"Okay."

"And don't try and convince me to go back to that house." He walked faster.

The house was farther away than Amelia thought it should be, and Morgan and Freely were very hard to see. She realized that she had to make a choice—Jack or them.

A scream rose up from the bleak landscape. Amelia looked toward its source and saw a thin, blond woman wearing a soiled, knee-length blue dress standing at the top of a low hill not far away. The woman was looking pleadingly at them, her arms outstretched.

"Jesus H. Christ!" Jack whispered.

The woman opened her mouth very wide, as if she were preparing to eat an apple whole, and screamed again.

"Jesus Fucking Christ!" Jack whispered again.

And the woman was swept away from them, into the dark air, arms still outstretched and mouth still opened wide. In moments, she was gone.

They stared at the spot where the woman had been. "The boy's mom," Amelia said.

"Yeah," said Jack. "His mom."

Amelia looked back. The house was gone.

Morgan and Freely were on their own.

Harry and Sam sat together at the bottom of the deep end of the heated pool and watched as the cops ran about above, pointing flashlights into the water. They could hear what were obviously shouted commands, but no individual words came through the twelve feet of water that separated them from the surface.

"I have to admit that it's good to see you," Harry said.

But Sam couldn't understand him through the water. He waved his hands in front of his face and pointed at his ears. Harry understood the gesture at once. He nodded, stood. "I've never breathed underwater before," he said.

Sam stood beside him and made the same gesture he'd made a moment earlier, to indicate that he couldn't understand what Harry was saying. Harry nodded again.

They walked side by side toward the shallow end. Halfway there, Harry stopped and, moving his lips in an exaggerated way so Sam would understand him, said, "They're going to see us."

Sam shook his head. "I don't think so."

Harry shrugged. "It doesn't matter anyway," he said.

They continued walking. Feeling the water move, they looked back. Someone in a brown suit had dived in and was frantically searching around the deep end. As they watched, someone else dove in and began looking too. For a moment, the man who had jumped in first looked their way but apparently saw nothing.

Harry grinned. "I feel like a spook!"

Sam tapped him on the shoulder and mouthed, "Did you say something?"

Harry shook his head and together they trudged from the pool.

Sydney awoke hungry, so he left the hotel and walked to a little Greek restaurant on Second Avenue, where he ordered ham and eggs and hashed browns, coffee, orange juice, pancakes and a side order of wheat toast.

The waitress, a thin woman with short brown hair and an eternal smile, explained that they didn't serve breakfast at night. She could get him the toast, she guessed, and the orange juice and coffee, but not the hashed browns, eggs or pancakes.

Sydney looked blankly at her for a minute, as if trying to understand what she'd told him, and when she began to explain it again—"I'm sorry, sir, but there's nothing I can do . . ."—he reached up from where he was sitting, grabbed her by the throat, growled, "That is unacceptable," and crushed her larynx.

She fell with a soft thud to the black and white tile floor and lay, trembling, on her back, mouth and eyes open, her order pad still clutched in her hand.

Several of the other diners saw all of this but stayed in their seats. One of them, a boy of fourteen, got the overwhelming urge to press a button and see the whole fascinating sequence of events again.

The owner of the restaurant, a short, stocky man with curly black hair, went for Sydney, who was still seated, with a fire extinguisher, the only weapon within easy reach.

"Our only hope is to keep walking," Amelia said.

"But it's so damned cold," Jack South protested. "And it ain't getting no warmer either."

"Tell me about it." She was hugging herself for warmth.

Snow began to fall on the bleak landscape.

"Jesus, snow!" Jack whispered.

260

It fell straight down because the air was so still.

"I'll bet it's ten degrees," Jack grumbled.

"Uh-huh," Amelia said.

"But since there's no wind," Jack added, "it feels like thirty." He forced a chuckle.

"Sorry?" Amelia said.

"Don't you get it? There's no wind, so it feels *warmer*."

She looked quizzically at him.

"Don't you remember," he explained, and began to walk faster, because the snow had started falling more heavily, "the weathermen were always saying things like, 'Well, it's five above, but with a fifteen-mile-an-hour wind, it feels like twenty below'?"

Amelia sighed. "Sure, I get it."

The snowflakes became as large as turtle shells.

"No wind," Amelia murmured.

"Yeah, no wind, so it feels like—"

"Shhh! I'm thinking."

Jack began to run.

"Goddammit!" she whispered, and ran after him. She easily caught up with him and grabbed his shoulder. He stopped running. "I didn't mean to offend you," she said.

"You didn't. I just figured I'd be warmer if I ran."

"Oh," she replied, and realized that he was right. "Well then, let's run."

It wasn't easy. The ground was pockmarked with exposed roots and irregularly shaped depressions. Jack fell twice, but quickly scrambled to his feet with Amelia's help.

"Where are we running to?" he asked as they ran.

"We're not running *to* anything," she told him. "We're running *from*."

"Are you sure?" he asked.

"No."

"And what about Morgan and Freely?"

"They'll have to fend for themselves, I'm afraid."

The snow stopped falling abruptly, as if it had been switched off.

The snow that had fallen was melting quickly. The air was growing warmer.

"Shit," Amelia said, "now he's going to try and cook us."

"That little kid, you mean?"

She nodded.

"You think *he's* doing all this?"

"Jack, get with the program. Of course he's doing it. It's his little space. Just like Silver Lake is my space and that . . . bunker is Conrad's space."

"And you really think that kid is changing the weather? You think he made it snow?"

"Within his own space, which this is, sure."

"Could *you* do it in your space?"

She thought about this and shook her head. "No. I couldn't. I tried, but I couldn't."

"The weather was just the weather, right? Like it always is."

"Yes, that's true," she said pointedly.

The temperature had risen into the sixties. It felt good.

"So what are you driving at, Jack?"

He shrugged. "I don't know what I'm driving at. I just think you think too much. Maybe you should stop thinking and just . . . stop thinking." He grinned.

Amelia sighed. Sometimes the observations of fools were simply that—foolish observations. She grimaced at the idea, suddenly disliking herself for it.

She nodded, "Yes, I know what you mean," she said, then realized that she sounded insincere.

Jack nodded glumly. "Sure you do," he said.

The temperature had climbed well into the seventies now. It still felt good, but neither Jack nor Amelia could enjoy it because it was rising so rapidly.

"It's almost like he wanted us to stop running," Jack said.

"I thought we agreed that the . . . little boy wasn't responsible for this?" Amelia said.

A flash of blue-green appeared at the close horizon. Then it was gone.

"The Octopus," Amelia whispered.

"Yeah," Jack agreed. "The Octopus. Reaching out."

"And reaching back."

Then, despite the rising temperature, they started to run again.

"One question," Harry said.

"Shoot."

Harry and Sam were walking side by side on an expressway that led from Chappaqua to the George Washington Bridge, and then to Manhattan. They were staying well on the shoulder, but traffic was whizzing by within inches. It was 10:30 P.M. and they'd been walking for an hour and a half.

"Actually, two questions," Harry corrected. "Maybe more."

"Shoot," Sam repeated.

"Why arc we walking?"

"To get to where we're going, I think," Sam answered.

"No, you don't understand. We're dead, right? I mean, we're spooks, spirits, ghosts, shades."

"Yes."

"Then why are we walking? Shouldn't we be able to . . . I don't know, fly? Levitate? *Wish* ourselves into being wherever we want to be?"

Sam shrugged. "If we could we would."

"Maybe we can."

Sam shook his head. "*I* can't. I've tried. I get *plooped*, sure, but that's not me doing it. It's someone else doing it."

"You mean God?"

A car sped past, horn blaring. "Hey," Harry declared, smiling, "I think he actually saw us."

"Some people can," Sam told him.

"But not everyone?"

"And it works the other way around too. We can't see all of the living."

"Why would that be?"

"I have no idea. You ask questions as if you expect me to give you answers. I don't have any answers, my friend. I'm like you. I just have questions."

"I've got an idea," Harry said. "Why don't we hitchhike." And he turned around, walked backward and stuck his thumb out.

"I think," Sam said, "that this is the way that great urban myths get started."

"Urban myths?"

"Sure. Remember the phantom hitchhiker? That's you now."

"Phantom, yeah." Harry smiled. He was beginning to enjoy himself. Being a spook in the real world was all right.

"Watch your feet there," Sam warned.

Harry looked at his feet. "Good Lord," he whispered. They were an inch into the pavement. "I'm sinking."

"No, just forgetting," Sam corrected.

A car sped past, then another, and another.

"Forgetting what?"

"That you're in a world you have no real business being in. You've got to *think* about things, Harry. Like where your feet should be."

"On top of the pavement, yeah, I know," Harry whispered, and his feet rose a bit, so he was again walking *on* the road and not *in* it. He glanced at Sam. "You mean I've got to think about this all the time?"

Sam nodded glumly. "Some part of you does, yes. And you've got to think about your clothes too, and your face and your muscles, your hair color, your eye color, whether your voice is coming out right—"

"Give me a break, Sam. Why do I have to do all that?"

"So the living who actually see you won't see something that makes them pee in their pants."

"You mean, without all this . . . physicalness we're really that frightening?"

"Trust me, Harry. We are."

An ancient Cadillac, bouncing on its springs and belching blue smoke, pulled over and stopped fifty yards ahead. The driver stuck his head out the driver's window and looked back. "Well, c'mon, before a cop sees us!" he called, and Harry and Sam ran to the car and climbed into the front seat.

Sydney had checked in at the Biltmore Hotel, on Second Avenue, and he was sleeping. He loved to sleep because his dreams were so entertaining and so delicious.

Ten stories below, Kennedy Whelan, his partner, Ian, another detective named Spears and two uniformed cops had gotten Sydney's room number from the desk clerk and were on their way up. The uniformed cops were taking the stairs, the detectives the elevator. Two other cops were on the street in front of the hotel and two more were in the alley behind, watching the fire escapes.

Chapter Thirty-four

"I saw it," Jack South whispered.

"Saw what?" Amelia asked.

"The car." With effort, he lifted his arm and pointed tremblingly at a narrow place between two low, bare hills several hundred yards ahead.

They'd stopped running. It was too hot and the air, foul with the smell of sulfur, was nearly too dense to breathe.

"Yes," Amelia said, "I think I saw it too." She wasn't sure of that. Perhaps it was simply wishful thinking. Who knew if they had even been heading in the right direction?

"Octopus," Jack said, thinking that if its tentacles were reaching, they would probably retract, and then he and Amelia would be free of this place.

"Yes," Amelia whispered. "Octopus."

They walked. Around them, the bleak landscape seemed to droop from the incredible heat. Branches of the bare, stunted trees drooped. The sky drooped with dollops of gray cloud. The spiky grasses that clumped on little hills drooped. The ground itself became soft and squishy underfoot.

"What good . . ." Jack wheezed, "is it . . . going to do us anyway?"

"You mean the car?"

He nodded.

Amelia said, "I don't know." She took a long breath. "We'll have to see."

The man driving the Cadillac was very talkative and very animated. He glanced at his two passengers often as he talked—which made Sam uneasy—and he also gesticulated wildly.

"So what's wrong with your friend there?" the man asked. "Does he always act like that?"

Sam glanced at Harry, who was staring straight ahead and sitting very stiffly. "What's wrong, pal?" Sam asked.

Harry shook his head quickly. "Just . . . concentrating," he answered.

"You don't have to concentrate that hard."

"What's he concentrating on?" the driver asked. "He looks like he's going to split a gut or something!"

"Harry, you don't really have to focus all of your energy like that."

"But . . . if I . . . don't—"

"Eventually, it'll become second nature."

"Jesus, look at him," the driver said. "He looks really spooky."

Sam smiled. So that's where the living got some of their ideas about the dead.

Sam whispered in Harry's ear, "You're a little stiff, my friend. Loosen up."

268

Harry whispered back, "What if I . . . float away or something?"

"I don't think that's going to happen."

"Is he sick?" the driver asked. "I got a barf bag there in the glove compartment if he's sick. Hell, I get sick all the time driving this thing. Bad exhaust. Leaks into the backseat, so I don't put no one there. But when I'm in traffic and I ain't movin', hell . . . Your friend need a barf bag?"

"No, I don't think so," Sam answered.

"One of these days, this damned car's going to kill me, I'm sure of it," the driver rattled on. "Am I driving too fast? I have to drive fast in order to keep the fumes behind me, you know. If I don't drive fast, then the fumes creep up here and make me sick. But if I'm driving *too* fast, you let me know. Some people don't like to drive fast. Me, I don't mind. I like it."

"No, it's all right," Sam said.

"Actually, it isn't—" Harry began.

"It's all right," Sam whispered to him. "It doesn't matter. We're going where we need to go."

"So you live in Chappaqua, huh?" the driver said. "Nice place. *Real* nice place. I lived in a place like that once. I lived in Chautauqua. That's downstate, near Erie, south of Buffalo. Nice place. Big houses. I like big houses. I guess I've always liked big houses. Big cars too. Well, that's obvious, ain't it? Nothing much bigger than this tank, huh? Yes, sir, big old Cadillac. Can't beat 'em. They stick to the road like tar. Barrel through the snow too."

Sam nodded to indicate the toll booths for the George Washington Bridge, several hundred yards ahead. The Cadillac was traveling over seventy miles an hour. "Aren't you going to stop?" he said.

269

"What? To pay a damned toll? Who stops to pay a damned toll?"

Sam dug in his pockets. "If you need a couple of quarters . . ." There were two kinds of toll booths, one manned by toll takers who made change and the other with a basket hung out for drivers to throw their quarters in.

The driver of the Cadillac waved his hand in the air. "Put your money away. You know what it is"— they were within fifty yards of the toll booths now and he hadn't slowed down—"it's, a matter of principle." They roared past the toll booths, suspension creaking, exhaust belching. Within seconds, sirens sounded and multicolored lights flashed behind them.

The driver laughed. "God, that's quite a show, ain't it! They spend more fucking money on electricity to run that alarm system than the damned toll is worth."

Sam looked back. A cop car pulled out of a parking area near the toll booths and came after them. "There's a cop after us."

Harry muttered, "Shit!"

The driver said, "It's not the first time. It won't be the last. Hell, I've had cops after me in twenty-five states. You run, they chase. It's a game. They like it. Everyone likes it. Gets put on one of those goddamned real-life crime shows and everyone thinks, Good, good, the police are doing their jobs! When *everyone*, fuck, *everyone* would love to run from the cops just once."

The police car was gaining on them fast.

"Maybe you should pull over," Sam suggested.

"My sentiments . . . exactly," Harry whispered.

"What'sa matter? You nervous?" the driver said, and laughed.

"Hey, it's all right. They never catch me. This

damned thing ain't like the wussy cars they're making today. It's got an *engine* in it!" He tromped the accelerator to the floor. The Cadillac took off like a rocket, leaving the cop car far behind.

Kennedy Whelan knocked on the door to room 8E at the Biltmore. A woman in her seventies opened the door after a few moments, saw Whelan with his gun drawn and shrieked.

"Goddammit!" Whelan muttered, and shouldered into the woman's room, pushing her in before him. He closed the door gently.

The woman shrieked again. Whelan took her hard by the shoulders, bent over, so he could look her in the eye, and said tightly, "I'm a cop!"

"No, you aren't!" she cried. "Prove it!"

Whelan withdrew his badge from his suit jacket pocket for her. She looked at it a moment, said, "Okay," and shrieked again.

"Goddammit!" Whelan repeated. Why hadn't Ian phoned all the other rooms first, as he'd been ordered? "Didn't you get a call?" Whelan asked.

"A call, a call?" she stammered. "What call? My phone's unplugged. I unplugged it."

"You unplugged it. Why?"

"So I could sleep, dammit!"

Whelan sighed. "Listen, all I want you to do is stay in your room and lock the door, okay?"

"Why? What's going on? Are you after someone? Is there going to be shooting?"

"Just, please, stay here and lock the door. Don't even go *near* the door, okay?"

"Why? Is someone going to shoot through it? Is that what's going to happen?"

271

"Just do as I ask. Please." He went to the door and stepped out into the hallway.

"Get back!" Ian barked.

Whelan snapped his head around and saw Ian at the end of the hall. He was gesturing frantically. "Ken, get back in that room!"

Whelan glanced in the opposite direction, toward room 8F, Sydney's room. He saw nothing.

He looked at Ian again, got another frantic gesture and tried the knob to room 8E. It was locked. He knocked on the door. "Open up!"

"No!"

He looked back at Ian and shrugged as if to ask what was happening.

"He's there!" Ian barked.

Whelan looked down the corridor but saw nothing.

"There!" Ian called. "Move!"

But as far as Whelan was concerned, the hallway was empty. He rapped on the door to room 8E once more.

"No!" the woman shrieked.

"Open the goddamned door!"

"Ken, watch out!" Ian called, and Whelan heard the quick, sharp snap of a .38 being fired—once, twice, again—followed by the loud, muffled thump of a .45 automatic from the other side of the hallway.

"What are you shooting at?" Whelan screamed. "What the fuck are you shooting at?"

He felt pressure on the back of his neck, instinctively fell to the floor and scrambled toward Ian, who, with Spears, was continuing to fire. "What the hell is going on?" Whelan yelled as he moved.

Ian fired again. His gun was empty. Whelan looked at him, saw him frantically begin to reload.

Spears continued firing.

"There's nothing there, goddammit, there's nothing there!" He was close to Ian now. "Stop shooting, there's nothing there!" he repeated.

Spears glanced at him wide-eyed and shook his head stiffly, as if in great confusion. He looked away and fired again.

Whelan saw a whisper of movement down the hall, as if the air were hot, but saw nothing else.

Spears coughed. Whelan swung around. Spears had his hands to his throat. His eyes were bulging, his mouth was halfway open and his tongue was sticking straight out. His skin had turned blue. He looked exactly as if he were choking himself.

Ian, within a few feet of Whelan, fired in Spears's direction.

"What in the hell are you doing?" Whelan barked, and leaped toward him, knocking him to the floor. The gun flew from Ian's hand. "Don't, don't," Ian stammered, and tried to wiggle out from beneath Whelan and retrieve his .38.

Spears crumpled to the floor with a great *Thud! Thump!*

The door to room 8E opened. The old woman stuck her head out into the hallway and shrieked.

Chapter Thirty-five

"Didn't I tell you?" the Cadillac driver bragged. "There's an *engine* in this thing. Didn't I tell you?"

Harry, still sitting stiffly, whispered, "He's a crazy man."

"What'd your friend say?" the driver growled.

"Maybe we should just get out of the car now," Sam suggested.

"What? You want to get out *here?*" the driver asked. They were in an abandoned area of the West Village and the Cadillac was moving very slowly through the darkness. The driver had turned the headlights out. "I do this all the time," he explained. "It makes me feel . . . covert."

"Sure, covert," Sam said.

"I'll take you wherever you want to go," the driver said. "You want to go uptown?"

"I think we'd like to make our own way from here," Sam told him.

"Make your own way where?"

"Wherever we're going," Sam answered.

The driver smiled coyly at him. "I know what you guys are up to," he announced.

"You do?" Sam asked.

"I'm so tired," Harry groaned.

"And I ain't scared," the driver said. "Maybe I should be. But I ain't. Like I said, I've run from cops in twenty-five states. I seen it all. Now I seen you." He grinned.

"Not everyone can," Sam told him.

"Not everyone can what?" the driver asked.

"See us."

"I'll bet," the driver said. "I'll bet. How about some music." He turned on the radio. Nothing happened. He scowled, muttered, "Goddamned thing" and hit the bottom of the dashboard with the palm of his hand. "Antenna connection's messed up. I should fix it, but who's got the time, right?" He hit the bottom of the dashboard again. Still nothing.

"It's all right," Sam said.

"I think we should get out," Harry whispered. "I'm not feeling well."

Sam looked quizzically at him.

"It's my head," Harry explained. "I feel light-headed."

"Of course you do," Sam said, smiling.

"It's not a joke," Harry said. "I feel like I'm about to faint."

"If he wants to puke," the driver said, "like I said, I got barf bags in the glove compartment." He came to a stop at a stop sign, looked dutifully right and left—which surprised the hell out of Sam—and pulled directly into the path of an oncoming street sweeper.

"Jesus Christ!" Sam breathed.

"What?" Harry whispered, gaze still riveted straight ahead.

The driver muttered, "Oh, shit!" at the same moment, and gunned the accelerator. But it was too late. With a sickening, metallic thud, the street sweeper slammed broadside into the Cadillac.

"It feels like we've been walking . . . for months," Jack South wheezed.

"Don't talk," Amelia told him. "Conserve your energy. I think we're making . . . progress."

The heat was incredible. Trees had become little green and brown puddles, like crayons left on a radiator. Spiky clumps of dark grasses looked like wet hair. The ground itself bore the consistency of pancake batter and made obscene oozing and sucking sounds as they pulled their feet through it.

"And you know what bugs me . . . most?" Jack said. "It don't bug me that I'm dead. What bugs me is, I didn't gain nothin' at all by dying."

"Please, Jack—"

"Like, I thought . . . well, I'm dead, it's a whole new . . . ball game, you know, a new . . . thing, a new start—"

"Conserve your strength, Jack."

"Shit, conserve my strength! Why? For what? So I can run the fucking . . . Boston Marathon?"

A flash of blue and green as quick and as startling as a lightbulb exploding brought them to a halt.

"Christ, what was that?" Jack said.

"He's losing it," Amelia said, smiling. "That was sky. We're almost where we want to be."

Jack said nothing.

"We've beaten him," Amelia gloated.

Another startling flash of sky.

"Maybe we've beaten him and maybe not," Jack whispered.

Another flash of blue and green. Then another, another and another, until the flashes were like strobe lights—startling, dizzying, disorienting.

Jack put his hand to his head, closed his eyes, sank to one knee on the hot earth.

Amelia squinted. She felt weakened by the light. Where was its source? Ahead? Behind? Above? Suddenly, those concepts meant nothing. The light was everywhere. And it was everything.

"He's trying to make us lose our way!" she shouted, as if, in the silence, the light itself were competing with her voice.

Jack lowered his head and stiff-armed the air, as if to push the light away.

"And we can't let him do it!" Amelia shouted. Her eyes were closed, but the light still insinuated itself, like the images in a fever dream.

She reached out and found Jack's chunky hand, yanking on it to coax him to his feet. "Please, Jack, don't give up now!" she pleaded. But her bravado, she knew, was senseless. She was blind because of the light. There were no drooping trees, no clumps of hairy grasses, no greedy, dark earth, no weeping sky. There was only the light. *His* light!

No, she realized. Not his light. His darkness *fighting* the light! And unless she and Jack found their way through that struggle and into the light itself, they would probably be lost in this place forever.

She yanked harder on his hand. "Jack, please!" But it was useless. He didn't want to move. She couldn't move him.

And it came to her that she had no choice. She had

to let him be. She had to leave him to fend for himself. Just as she had had to leave Morgan and Freely. For God's sake, Jack wasn't *stupid!* What right did she have to assume that he needed her more than she needed him? That was . . . elitist bullshit!

Rationalization! she realized. She wanted to leave him behind now, because she wanted to save herself. If he wasn't up to aiding in his own rescue, then he wasn't worth rescuing.

She grabbed his wrist with her free hand, so she was holding him with both hands, and pulled with all her strength. It was like pulling on a tree stump.

She opened her eyes. The light overwhelmed her. She saw nothing.

She closed her eyes. "Jack, I don't want to leave you here!" she shouted.

But she did want to leave him here, she realized. She wanted desperately to save herself. She let go of his hand and ran blindly through the light.

The operator of the street sweeper stared wide-eyed at the driver of the Cadillac and murmured, "Oh, Lord, what have I done now?"

Sam looked at the man and said, "Can you see me?"

The man said nothing.

"He can't see us," Harry said.

The man reached into the broken driver's window of the Cadillac and patted the driver's face gently. The collision had knocked the Cadillac onto its back. "Hey, mister, you're all right, ain'tcha?"

But the driver wasn't all right. Three of his cervical vertebrae had been cracked when he'd fallen to the roof of the car. "Ambulance," he mouthed.

The operator of the street sweeper reached in with

his other hand and grabbed the driver by the shoulder. "It's okay, fella. I'll get you out of there!"

"Idiot!" Sam yelled. "Don't do that!"

But the man did it anyway, and as he did, he dragged the driver's neck over a twisted section of the car's metallic window frame, lacerating his jugular vein.

The driver was dead two minutes later.

Harry and Sam scrambled from the passenger's side of the car and started walking again.

"Bad experience," Harry said as they went along. He was staring at his feet, making sure he didn't sink into the sidewalk.

"More for him than for us," Sam said.

"Do you think it means anything?" Harry asked.

"Like what?"

"That we're ... I don't know ..." He shrugged. "The kiss of death?"

"That's stupid," Sam told him.

Harry glanced at him. "No, it isn't."

"We have no proof." Sam nodded. "Harry, you're floating."

Harry looked quickly at his feet. "Jesus, I am!" He was a foot above the sidewalk.

"And you're ... losing yourself," Sam went on.

"Losing myself?" He looked down at his torso, his arms, his legs.

"Stop levitating first, before someone sees you."

Harry concentrated on the sidewalk and within moments was only an inch or so above it. "That's the best I can do," he explained. "I feel so damned ... tired. I feel like someone's ... I don't know, *tugging* at me."

"You need a nose," Sam told him.

Reflexively, Harry put his hand to his nose. "But I

279

can feel it." He looked cross-eyed at it. "And I can see it too."

"Well, *I* can't!" Sam declared, but then, suddenly, he could see it again, because Harry had concentrated on it. Sam went on, "You're not very good at this, are you?"

"Maybe I'm just not as practiced as you are."

"Yeah, maybe."

"And I think I'll get better at it in time. If I *have* time."

"Sure you do. And you will."

They turned a corner and blundered into heavy pedestrian traffic. People were moving briskly about, bustling here and there—to little bookstores that stayed open late, to coffee shops, bakeries, restaurants, doors opening and closing. They moved in the way that New Yorkers move—with purpose and agility.

There were singles and couples—man, woman; man, man; woman, woman—although few children and old people.

"I've always liked it here," Harry said.

"Yeah, it's all right," Sam agreed grudgingly.

They stopped walking. They had no idea where they were going exactly and they needed a moment to consider their situation.

"We know that Sydney's in New York City somewhere," Harry said.

"Yeah, we know that."

"And my guess is that if we just . . . set our minds to it—"

"No, no," Sam cut in. "I don't believe that's going to work. It's a Zen thing, I think."

Harry looked curiously at him. "A Zen thing?

Somehow, I find it odd to hear that phrase coming from you."

Around them, people continued bustling here and there. There was lots of talking, but it was of the close, confidential kind, as if the private lives of these people meshed with the tone of the place, but not loudly.

"C'mon, Harry," Sam protested, "how could I *not* know what a *Zen thing* is?"

Harry shrugged. "So tell me how it's going to help us find Sydney?" he asked. "Is that the way you worked when you were alive? Did you go after . . . errant husbands that way?"

"There was a lot of legwork, a lot of paperwork, a lot of questions to be asked. I don't know exactly *how* we're going to find Sydney. Maybe we're going to have to let him find us."

"That means sticking around, doesn't it?"

"Sticking around?"

"Here. In New York City."

Sam nodded. "I think so. I don't know for how long. A while. If Sydney's been killing people, then the cops are looking for him too. We'll just follow them."

Harry shook his head. "I don't think I've got the time for that, Sam." He paused. "Actually, I don't think I've got any time at all. I feel like I'm . . . imploding." He gave Sam a feeble smile. "And I feel so exhausted. Something doesn't want me to be here, Sam." He shrugged. "I feel like I simply don't exist."

When he shrugged, he levitated a few inches and his right arm disappeared. "Harry," Sam warned, "you're losing it."

Harry grimaced and was quickly whole and earthbound again. "I don't think I'll ever get the hang of this," he said. "I just feel so damned tired."

"Did I see what I think I saw?" a woman behind them asked.

Sam turned toward the woman's voice. She was tall, athletically built, short-haired and red-cheeked, and she was wearing a gray, skin-tight exercise suit that seemed very much out of place this winter night. As she spoke, she jogged in place and smiled at the same time, as if at a feat of magic she couldn't figure out. "Did you just . . . float?" she asked Harry.

He shook his head a little and muttered, "No. Of course not. No one can float."

"But *you* can. I saw it. You're better than David Copperfield." She continued jogging in place.

"Actually," Sam explained, "it was only an illusion."

"Of course it was only an illusion," she said, still smiling, though her tone was scolding. "I know that."

"Aren't you cold?" Sam asked, nodding at her exercise outfit.

"You keep moving, you don't get cold," she said. "So, go ahead, do it again. I'll pay you."

"You'll pay him?" Sam said incredulously.

"Sure. I don't have any money on me at the moment." Her smile broadened. "Well, that's obvious, isn't it."

Sam felt himself blushing.

"But I will pay you," she went on.

"No, thanks," Harry said, and then to Sam, "C'mon, let's get going. We've got a killer to find."

"Please, don't go," the jogger said. "I didn't mean to . . . offend you. Did I offend you?"

Sam shook his head. "It's all right. We're in a hurry."

"Everyone's in a hurry," she scolded. "Even me."

She stopped jogging in place. "Okay, if you're not going to levitate again, I'm going to stand here until I freeze to death."

"No, you aren't," Sam said, and he and Harry turned away from her and started walking again.

"But I am, I will!" the woman called after them.

Sam said, "I think we can safely assume that the people who see us aren't normal."

"Yeah, I've noticed," Harry said.

Sam felt someone tapping him on the shoulder. He stopped, turned. The jogger was there. "Okay, so I won't freeze myself to death," she said, smiling. "Just tell him to levitate again, okay?"

Sam sighed, looked at Harry and said, "Levitate, Harry."

"I wish I could," Harry said, but then he did. He rose half a foot, hesitated, rose another foot, two feet, three feet, while the jogger watched, wide-eyed and openmouthed.

"Uh, Sam," Harry said tentatively, when he stopped rising at about the level of Sam's elbow, "I don't think I can come back down."

"Shit," Sam muttered.

"I'm thinking about the sidewalk, but it doesn't work. I'm too damned tired to concentrate." He glanced about at the people bustling here and there. "This is humiliating."

The jogger looked about quickly, then whispered, "Why doesn't anyone . . . else . . . see him?"

Sam considered her question a moment and answered, "Because he's not really there. You've got . . . toys in your attic and he's one of them."

"He must be," she breathed. "My God, I'm nuts. I knew it was going to happen sooner or later. I could see the signs. Talking to myself. All this . . . jogging.

Too many endorphins. Too much pleasure." She smiled again. "But you know what? It's all right. At least I'm not seeing bug-eyed monsters crawling on the ceiling. I'm seeing a levitating man in a trench coat." Her eyebrows furrowed. "Hey, what's he supposed to be anyway?"

"A detective," Sam answered.

She nodded. "Yeah. Fits. Detective. I like detectives. Sam Spade, Philip Marlowe. Sure. I go nuts and I see levitating detectives. It's all kind of . . . primal, I think." She gave Sam a once-over. "But how about you? Why am I seeing you too?"

"So I can explain *him*," Sam answered at once.

"I can explain myself," Harry managed wearily from above.

"Don't get testy," the jogger scolded. "I think your friend has a point. I think what he represents is my . . . weird but rational self explaining my weird but irrational self to my pragmatic self. We're all trilateral. Look at *The Three Faces of Eve*. Why *three*? Because she was trilateral. We're all trilateral." Her smile broadened. "I'm so happy I met you two. Really. Now I can get in touch with my true self at last."

And with that, she turned away and jogged off, straight into an opening glass door. She crashed through it and fell face forward onto the sidewalk, glass shards cascading and blood pooling at various points around her body.

Sam said, "I'm afraid you were right, my friend."

"Yeah," Harry sighed from above. "We *are* the kiss of death."

Sleepeasy

Chapter Thirty-six

Amelia couldn't guess how long she'd been running blind—afraid to see—through the fields of nodding sunflowers, under that flat blue-green sky, before she dared to open her eyes and stop running. It could have been hours. The bleak landscape where she'd left Morgan and Freely and Jack South was probably miles away—who knew in what direction?—and she supposed that she had no real hope of finding them again.

She was on her own.

And perhaps, after all, that was precisely as things were meant to be. Here. In this place. This afterlife. Perhaps it was a place where she was supposed to confront herself at last. A place where she was supposed to define herself from her creations. A place where she would learn, most importantly, that she had no control over them.

Or maybe that was all just more bullshit. More rationalization. She'd run out on her friends and now she was trying to make excuses for it.

If so, this was an exquisite punishment for that cowardice. Lost in God only knew how many square miles of sunflowers and sky. No monster Buick, no quirky people, no lake, no pleasant existence in which she confronted nothing but warm days and cool nights.

Well, for Christ's sake, she sure as hell was confronting *nothing* now. Acres and acres and acres of it.

She sighed, sat down yoga-style on the fertile earth, smelled clay—a familiar smell. She put her elbows on her knees, propped her head on her palms and stared straight ahead. There were sunflowers stalks everywhere she looked. They were like the individual hairs on a giant's head.

"Shit," she whispered. If only she had the road. The Buick. Even the Buick without its blessed air-conditioning.

Then she did. She shrieked in surprise. The Buick sat a dozen feet away, on a rutted dirt road that snaked off into the endless square miles of sunflower fields.

She looked about and smiled. So that was it. The sunflowers themselves were the spaces in the emptiness. The wishing spaces. Good Lord, Morgan and Freely and Jack Smith could be building their own existence at that very moment if only she'd realized this basic fact.

She would have to find them. Somehow, she'd have to find them.

She stood, swiped at the seat of her white shorts, went to the Buick and climbed into the driver's seat. She felt for the ignition. No keys. Goddammit! She needed the car keys. How was she going to go anywhere without them? And as she thought this, the keys appeared in the ignition.

"Good," she whispered, starting the Buick. She flicked on the switch for the air-conditioning. Nothing.

Dammit to hell. She couldn't drive through this heat without air-conditioning. She *needed* air-conditioning.

She smiled again. That wish had probably done the trick. She flicked the air-conditioning switch off, then on. Still nothing. She frowned. So that's the way it was. She'd been right. One wish to a customer.

She got out of the Buick, slammed the door and stalked off, until she was well into the sunflowers again and couldn't see the rutted road, or the Buick.

She sat down again and put her head in her palms. Gee, she thought, it would be great to have a Corvette on a four-lane highway.

Nothing. The sunflowers kept nodding at her.

Dammit to hell, it would really be great, she thought, to have a Corvette on an empty four-lane highway that took me anywhere I wanted to go!

Still nothing. She stood. So *that's* the way it was! She looked about. Where in the hell had she left the Buick? She mentally retraced her steps. Had she turned around before sitting down? Had she gone right or left after leaving the road behind?

"Oh, hell," she whispered. She'd really put her foot in it this time.

A metallic flash caught her eye through the sunflowers. She ran toward it and within minutes was seated behind the Buick's steering wheel. She rolled the window down, started the engine and was on the road again.

*   *   *

Kennedy Whelan was tired of answering questions. So many questions. So few answers.

"No one was there," he said, for what seemed like the thousandth time. "Spears choked himself to death. It's the fucking truth!" His rear end had fallen asleep from sitting so long.

"I'm sorry, Ken," said the officer from internal affairs. "But that sort of thing just doesn't happen, does it?"

"Yes, it does happen. I saw it."

"The past twenty-four hours have been pretty . . . strange, haven't they, Ken?"

"Get to the point."

"The point is, you've been under a lot of stress. This guy you say was connected with our Sydney Greenstreet character jumps into his own pool and disappears. I don't know how it happened. *You* don't know how it happened. But it happened. So when you tell me that Spears and your partner both choked themselves to death—"

"I didn't say that Ian choked himself to death."

"Correct. You didn't. But he's dead, his throat was crushed, same as Spears—"

"Please, just let me go home. I need some sleep. I'm tired, for Christ's sake." He pulled a cigar from his pocket and stuck it into his mouth without lighting it.

"Sorry, Ken. The shrink wants to see you first."

"Fuck that. She can talk to me later. Tomorrow." He stood. "Now, unless you're actually charging me—"

"Of course we're not charging you, Ken. We just have a lot of questions that need answering and apparently you're the only one that can answer them. Hell, we've got two dead cops, another cop who's apparently walking a thin line between sanity and insanity, and a madman loose in the city—"

"There are lots of madmen loose in the city," Whelan interrupted, then, punctuating his words by jabbing the air with his cigar, he added, "No one can catch them all!" And with that, he scooped up his jacket from the back of the chair, left the room and went out to his car to drive home.

"I think you're doing this to be funny," Sam said, and glanced at Harry, still walking at the level of his elbow.

"I wish I were," Harry said. "I wish I had that ability. I'd give anything to have that ability. But it's like I'm at the mercy of . . . *something*—"

Plooped! Sam thought.

"Like when you get thrown back and forth in time," Harry went on. "Don't you feel that something's . . . I don't know, having its way with you?"

"Yeah, I do," Sam said glumly. "It's like something . . . some*one*—who knows who, maybe God, for Christ's sake?—is having fun with me. And I'll tell you, my friend, I don't like it."

"Well, that's the way I feel now, Sam. Like I'm being made the butt of a joke. The way Amelia—I mean Barbara—always did. Even when she was alive. Something is picking me up off the sidewalk and holding me in midair. Because I really am thinking about the surface of that damned sidewalk, Sam. Trust me on this." A quick pause. "I just feel so damned tired. I can't explain it."

An ambulance roared past, siren blaring.

"Poor woman," Sam said.

"Maybe we'll see her again," Harry said.

"Yeah, that's what I'm afraid of."

"And the driver of the Cadillac too."

Sam nodded. "What a crazy world we live in."

Harry managed a grin. Sam was being ironic.

Sydney itched. He scratched and scratched, but the itch remained. He scratched everywhere. On his arms, his legs, his chest, his bald head, his nose. Everything itched.

Sydney had never itched before, so this was something awful and new. And as he scratched and scratched furiously, he thought that pieces of himself were shredding and falling off. When he scratched the back of his hand, he felt certain that the skin was falling off in strips. And when he scratched at his chest, he felt just as certain that his black suit was splitting and tearing under his fingernails. But when he looked, he saw that it wasn't so. His hand was whole. His suit was whole. *He* was whole. He simply itched abominably.

Around him, on Second Avenue, there were people who gasped, pointed and screamed at him as he walked and scratched and itched. Still others wanted desperately to know what the fuss was all about.

"What in the hell is going on?" someone said.

"Good Lord, can't you see him?"

"See who?"

"Him! That . . . man . . . coming apart!"

"And when we *do* find him—if we find him—what are we going to do with him?" Sam asked.

Harry, still walking at Sam's elbow, could not answer the question. He shook his head, tried to think of a philosophical approach to the subject, could think of nothing. All of his concentration was on staying just where he was, and perhaps that—his intense, con-

tinuous, single-minded effort to stay earthbound—
was responsible for the incredible exhaustion he felt.
But if he couldn't walk on the sidewalk, as Sam was,
he could at least stay a few feet above it, although
even that was becoming difficult. Something was tugging very hard on him from above and he felt like a
marionette.

"Well," Sam coaxed, "are you going to answer
me?"

"I can't," Harry admitted. "I don't know *what*
we're going to do with him."

"Shit. You created him, my friend. You should sure
as hell be able to control him—"

"The way you controlled that . . . thing that at-
tacked our boat?"

Sam glanced up at him, surprised. "How'd you
know?"

Harry shrugged. "I may not be able to keep my feet
on the ground, Sam, but it doesn't mean I'm stupid."
He rose a bit further, to the level of Sam's neck, as
he said this. "Goddammit," he whispered, and sank
to his previous level.

Two blocks up, Sam noticed that a car had stopped
halfway into the intersection. It was an odd place to
stop, he thought.

"Look at that!"

"Yes," Harry replied. "I see him."

"And I think he sees us," Sam said. As he was
speaking, the car shot through the intersection and
sped toward them, horn blasting so that traffic and
pedestrians would get out of its way.

"Shit!" Harry breathed.

"This way," Sam called, turning to his left and running down an alley.

Harry—six, seven, eight feet off the sidewalk—

followed, though clumsily. When he tried to run, his feet slid, as if he were running on ice. Sam quickly outdistanced him and within moments was at the far end of the alley, fifty yards away.

"Sam, I can't do it!" Harry yelled, and heard a car come to a grinding halt on the street, heard a door slam.

He was close to one of the two brick buildings that formed the alley's walls. He groped for the wall, a few feet away, but his hand went into it. He quickly withdrew it, cursing.

From ten feet below, he heard, "What are you doing, Mr. Briggs?"

He looked. Kennedy Whelan was scowling up at him.

"Come down from there, goddammit!"

Harry shook his head vigorously. He didn't want to speak, out of fear that actual dialogue with Whelan would doom the man. He glanced at Sam—looking on from the end of the alley—and back at Whelan. He shook his head once more.

"You're playing some kind of game, Mr. Briggs," Whelan growled, "and I don't like it. I don't have either the time or the patience for it."

Harry shook his head again. Out of the corner of his eye, he saw Sam approaching from the end of the alley.

"Sam, please, stay there!" he shouted.

Whelan looked down the alley. His brow furrowed. He drew his .38 from his shoulder holster and pointed it at Sam. "That's far enough, mister," he shouted. "Now get down on your belly, arms and legs spread."

Sam kept coming.

"Goddammit," Whelan shouted, "I *will* fire on you if you don't get on your belly now!"

Sam kept coming.

Whelan cocked his .38. "You've got five seconds to get down or I'll fire. One, two—"

Sam kept coming.

"Three—"

Sam disappeared.

Whelan fired. Once, twice, again. With his gun still held out on his extended arms, he whispered, "Where the fuck is he?" glanced at Harry, then back at the empty alley. "Where the fuck did he go?"

And Harry, despite himself, despite what he believed were the awful effects of dialogue with the living, said "Plooped," and then consciously forgot all about the sidewalk, the brick buildings, the alley, Whelan, Sydney.

At that, he drifted off into the New York City winter air.

Chapter Thirty-seven

Amelia wondered if she would *want* to go back to Silver Lake, even if she knew how to get there. Her quirky but pleasant people had clearly been in the process of changing when she'd left. She might return and discover that she had become *persona non grata* with them and wasn't welcome in the very place that she'd created. But the question was probably hypothetical anyway. She had no idea where she was. How could she? Around her, nothing but nodding sunflowers crowded the narrow road. Hours earlier, she'd passed an idyllic little house, complete with gingerbread. A big red barn stood beside it. A horse leaped about in a pasture near the barn, and a woman and child watched blankly from the house's porch as she sped past. She hadn't felt the need to stop. Let them have their dreams, for as long as they were allowed. And when those dreams began to change and take on a life of their own, that mother and child would deal with them as well as they could. It seemed to be the way that things worked here. God knew why.

For now, she would simply continue driving. If this place had boundaries, perhaps she would reach them sooner or later. If this place was actually *run* by someone, perhaps she'd bump into him—or her—sooner or later and then she'd pepper him—or her—with questions.

Or perhaps, sooner or later, she'd find Morgan and Freely and Jack South. Perhaps they'd have built some spaces of their own and would have learned to cope with their creations.

And maybe she'd find Harry too. She smiled. She realized that she actually *wanted* to find him and that surprised her. In life, their relationship had been so combative, so unpredictable, so volatile. But now she missed him and wanted him with her. Perhaps putting the seconds, minutes and hours, the days, years and decades behind her would, all by itself, accomplish that.

She turned on the radio. Harry Chapin, "Time in a Bottle." She smiled again. All she ever seemed to pick up here were dead people singing pertinent songs. Whoever ran this place was as corny as Kansas in August.

Sydney was unimportant. Sam Goodlow was unimportant. Whelan was unimportant. Even Amelia, Silver Lake and the murder of the uninvolved were unimportant. And he, Harry Briggs—whoever he might have been—was unimportant . . .

Only sleep mattered. Blissful, deep and unencumbered. He was entitled. Everyone became entitled after a lifetime of pain and doubt.

Far below, the lights of Manhattan winked out, one

by one, until the city was dark. As it joined with the dark sky, Harry felt a cold hand in his and heard a soothing voice tell him, "This way."

He questioned nothing. He let himself be carried off.

Sam Goodlow looked out of Viola Pennypacker's living-room window and saw the people gathered on the beach only a stone's throw away. There were half a hundred people, all naked and animated, laughing, talking, running, swimming and making love in the bright daylight.

Sam blushed because of all the wagging fannies and bouncing breasts and erect cocks he was seeing. Was this, he asked himself incredulously, the community that Harry's wife had created?

He moved away from the window, hesitated, then went to the front door and opened it. He stepped out onto the porch and hesitated again. He felt uncertain and a little afraid, though he wasn't sure why.

A young woman on the beach turned, saw him, stared. He stared back. Then, almost as one, the rest of the people on the beach turned and stared at him too. He returned their gaze.

A young man took a few steps toward him. A young woman nearby did the same, and then an old couple, an old woman, another young woman, a child. The whole group was moving slowly and deliberately his way, gazes fixed and unblinking.

Sam stared back. Fear made his stomach turn over.

The room was as big as a football stadium and it held thousands and thousands of people who were lying on their backs on what might have been legless slabs of pine. Harry guessed that they were sleeping.

He saw these people dimly because the room was dimly lit. He heard no snoring and no breathing. No one talked while they slept. No one rolled over or rolled back, or got up to pee or thrashed about, victimized by insomnia.

Everyone slept without sheets, blankets, pillows and pajamas. They slept close to one another. Backs of hands touched backs of hands. Ankles touched ankles, thighs, ears. Hair intruded, with protest from no one, upon bellies, chests, forearms.

Harry wanted to join these people, he *needed* to join them. But when he looked about, he saw no free space. He sensed that someone was standing with him in the room, although he could see only the sleeping bodies on their slabs. He patted himself at his hips, his chest. He was still wearing his trench coat and double-breasted suit. This wasn't right. How could he sleep in his clothes?

A voice as neutral and as sexless as air told him, "You have a choice." The voice was not at his right or left shoulder. It wasn't beneath, above or in front of him. "You could choose to sleep, as these people have. And if that's your choice, then you'll sleep just as they are. Completely. And without interruption."

"Are you saying that I'll sleep forever?" Harry asked.

"Or you may choose to return," the voice went on. "And if you do that, then you'll never sleep."

"Return?" Harry asked. "To where?"

"If you sleep," the voice said, "all that you've created in this life will sleep too."

"This life? Which life?" Harry asked. "And what do you mean 'all that I've created'? Do you mean Sydney?"

"And if you return," the voice said, "all that you've

created in this life will return with you."

"I don't know what in the hell you're talking about," Harry pleaded. "I'm just so damned tired."

"And this is the place for sleep," the voice said.

"Forever?" Harry repeated.

"What's forever?" the voice said.

"It will be exactly like being dead, won't it?" Harry asked.

"It depends upon your point of reference, I suppose," the voice said.

Point of reference, Harry thought. Sure, everything depended upon one's "point of reference." The universe was cluttered with bullshit. He couldn't avoid it, even here.

But in reality and despite the bullshit, he realized that he had no real choice. If he returned (to what and to where?), he would drag Sydney along with him. If he stayed here and . . . slept, then Sydney would sleep too. So what real choice did he have? If he chose to return, then he was probably choosing death for who knew how many other people, because of *his* creation. If he stayed here, it would be the classic *That's all there is, there ain't no more!* kind of death for himself, and for Sydney. His choice was obvious.

"I'm staying," he announced, feeling at once very noble and very afraid.

"But you're not sure," the voice taunted.

"I *want* to stay," Harry declared.

"Those who choose sleep, must be certain. You simply aren't."

"I'm certain that I'm exhausted," Harry said.

"That's not enough," the voice said.

"People get exhausted, they sleep, dammit!" Harry protested.

"You think I'm going to argue with you?" the voice

said. "Exhaustion isn't enough. You haven't stopped living, so you have no place here. Sorry. My mistake."

And with that, the huge room with its endlessly sleeping people was gone.

Sam thought very briefly about going back into Viola Pennypacker's house, locking the door and hiding, but he decided that if he did that, he'd be stuck there for God knew how long. So he ran.

And the inhabitants of Silver Lake came after him. En masse. Silently and single-mindedly. Like cats. Leonard, Mrs. Conte, Mrs. Alexander, Gilly and half a hundred others. Gazes fixed and unblinking. Their naked bodies glistening nicely in the bright daylight.

He ran from cottage to cottage, banged on doors, got no answer, kept running. He didn't know what these people wanted from him, but he wasn't about to stop and ask.

It occurred to him, all at once, that it was likely they just wanted him to leave. He stopped running and looked at them. They were only a few yards away. He thought he'd been faster.

"Okay, okay, I'm leaving," he told them.

They stared silently at him.

"Really, I'm leaving," he repeated. "I know when I'm not welcome." He attempted a smile.

They stayed put. They said nothing.

He looked around. What was the quickest way out of this place?

"Maybe you could help me," he suggested.

They only stared.

He nodded. "Sure, I understand. I'll find my own way."

He turned. A footpath led around the side of a neat

301

little cottage nearby and then into a small stand of trees. He pointed, looked back. "This way, huh?"

The inhabitants of Silver Lake said nothing. He took the path into the woods.

Doodling in Time

Chapter Thirty-eight

The man boarding the 129th Street subway train usually paid no more attention to graffiti than any other subway rider. It was as ubiquitous as bad air or lousy manners. But this bit of graffiti—scrawled in scab-red near the subway car's rear door—caught his brief attention because it seemed so earnest, and so anachronistic too. Modern graffiti artists weren't so much interested anymore in declaring their existence and importance through their names and a few four-letter words as in constructing elaborate and delicate structures in pastel that they coaxed from inexpensive cans of spray paint.

SYDNEY WAS HERE! the graffiti read, and the sub way rider—with a fondness for simpler times—smiled nostalgically at it before boarding the train.

The woman using the stall in the third-floor Macy's powder room closed the door, sat down, then shrieked. The words SYDNEY WAS HERE! were scrawled in scab-red on the inside of the stall door.

The phrase appeared again and again throughout Manhattan. On doors and windows, on statues, sidewalks, roadways and street signs. On bridges, boats and even in the corners of a few placards that advertised free film and topless dancing. SYDNEY WAS HERE!

Few who saw the phrase actually read it or registered it. There were some who saw it in more than one place and some who actually saw it in half a dozen places. But few of these people took any more notice of it than they did the sleeping homeless, who were also ubiquitous, or the thousands of cooing pigeons underfoot, or the yellow cabs that zipped here and there. SYDNEY WAS HERE!—emblazoned everywhere in scab-red—was simply another one of countless minor annoyances that seemed to erupt overnight. Eventually, people would be dispatched to scrub it away wherever it appeared.

Harry Briggs had been driving for a long time on a road that seemed to snake endlessly through fields of tall grass and nodding sunflowers. He wasn't sure how long he'd been driving. It seemed like centuries. He'd stopped for coffee and for meals—at friendly little restaurants that rose up magically from the fields of tall grass and sunflowers—and he'd stopped to stretch his legs, but he hadn't stopped to sleep and he thought that he should be getting tired by now. He supposed that it was midafternoon when he decided this, and that he was sweating because the road that cut through the nodding sunflowers and tall grass was supernaturally hot.

He didn't notice until the deed was done that a fat, black spider had crawled up from somewhere inside the car's front seat and bitten him on his bare forearm. He saw the spider—it was staring at him with tiny red eyes—and he saw the slight discolored area on his arm, so he hit the brake pedal and pulled over to the shoulder of the road.

"Jesus," he whispered, not because the bite hurt, but because it was so unsettling to be bitten and not have noticed right away. It was unsettling also to have huge black spiders living inside his car's front seat. There might be dozens of spiders in there. Aunt and uncle spiders, mother and father spiders, baby spiders waiting to grow up. A whole community of fat spiders with tiny red eyes.

He stared at the spider that was staring at him from his bare forearm—gripping the steering wheel—and he realized that he didn't know what to do. Perhaps the spider merely wanted light and air. Blood and companionship. So it had staked a claim to his forearm, and if he, Harry, tried to uproot it, it would probably bite him again.

"You can't stay there," Harry said, and the creature moved its huge front legs a little, as if in response. At last, it lumbered off, down his forearm and into the seat again.

When he looked up again, he saw that the shadows had lengthened and that dusk, like a shower of fire, was upon him.

Harry showed a photograph to the cashier at a natural foods store and asked if she had ever seen the person in the photograph. The woman answered that she hadn't, then added, "But there are so many people coming and going these days. It's like a parade."

Harry said, "Thanks, anyway," and bought some of the woman's natural foods, because he felt duty-bound to now that he had taken up her time.

He stopped at a gas station and showed the man tending the pumps the same photograph. The man looked at it for a moment and said, "She's one classy dame, ain't she?" Harry agreed, but then the man went on to say that he had never seen her before and that even if he had, he probably wouldn't remember her, considering how "crowded the roads have been." Harry frowned, said thanks, put $5 worth of gasoline into his monster Buick—though he didn't need the gasoline—and drove off.

Presently, he stopped to pick up a hitchhiker. Harry had done a lot of hitchhiking and he knew how it felt to stand in the heat or the cold for hours at a time waiting for a ride.

"Where you headed?" he asked the stocky, craggy-faced, red-haired man he'd picked up.

"I really don't know, Harry," the man answered, though Harry hadn't told him his name. "And I'd say the same about you too."

Harry supposed that this answer should have made him uncomfortable. He supposed it should even have sounded a little threatening. But it didn't, because he got the notion that he had met this man before. Harry asked him, "Do I know you?"

"We know each other," the man answered.

Harry glanced at the man and nodded. "Yes," he said, "I think we do." But he couldn't imagine from where or when.

"I like your getup," the man said.

"My getup?" Harry repeated.

"Yeah. Your detective getup. I like it."

"Thanks," Harry said.

As they drove through the nodding sunflowers, under the blue-green sky, another hitchhiker appeared. He was fat and he wore a black suit and a wide silver tie.

"Look at him!" Harry proclaimed. "My God, he looks just like Sydney Greenstreet."

"Pass him by," the red-haired man said.

"I can't do that. It's hot out there."

"Trust me on this."

Harry glanced at the red-haired man, saw how earnest he was and kept going. Strangely, Harry *did* trust him.

Eventually, another hitchhiker appeared. He was tall, clean-shaven, tired-looking and he had a big cigar hanging from his mouth.

"Him too," said the red-haired man.

"He looks like a cop," Harry said.

"That's because he is a cop," said the red-haired man. "And my guess is he's pretty upset."

"How would you know that?"

"I know some things that you don't, my friend. Or maybe they're things you've simply forgotten."

Again, Harry saw how earnest the red-haired man was, so he nodded and kept going. "I suppose I've forgotten as much in this life as anyone has," he said, smiling.

"It will all come back to you in time," said the red-haired man.

A few minutes later, Harry took out the photograph he'd been showing around and handed it to his companion. "I'm looking for this woman. Maybe you can help me. Her name is . . ." He faltered. "Her name is . . ." He stopped.

"Yes?" coaxed the red-haired man. "What's her name?"

"Amelia," Harry answered. "Her name's Amelia," he said resolutely. Another smile, broad and bright, as if he had stumbled upon some truth that had long eluded him. "Her name's Amelia." He glanced at the red-haired man. "Have you seen her?"

"You've been looking for her for a long time?" asked the red-haired man.

"It seems like centuries," Harry answered.

"Then we'll look for her together, my friend."

Harry glanced at him, then back at the road, the nodding sunflowers, the clear, blue-green sky. This was such a vast and lonely and unpredictable place. It would be good to have company.

"Yes," he said. "Together. I think I'd like that."

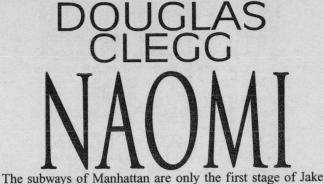

DOUGLAS CLEGG
NAOMI

The subways of Manhattan are only the first stage of Jake Richmond's descent into the vast subterranean passageways beneath the city—and the discovery of a mystery and a terror greater than any human being could imagine. Naomi went into the tunnels to destroy herself . . . but found an even more terrible fate awaiting her in the twisting corridors. And now the man who loves Naomi must find her . . . and bring her back to the world of the living, a world where a New York brownstone holds a burial ground of those accused of witchcraft, where the secrets of the living may be found within the ancient diary of a witch, and where a creature known only as the Serpent has escaped its bounds at last.

___4857-4 $5.99 US/$6.99 CAN

YOU COME WHEN I CALL YOU

DOUGLAS CLEGG

An epic tale of horror, spanning twenty years in the lives of four friends—witnesses to unearthly terror. The high desert town of Palmetto, California, has turned toxic after twenty years of nightmares. In Los Angeles, a woman is tormented by visions from a chilling past, and a man steps into a house of torture. On the steps of a church, a young woman has been sacrificed in a ritual of darkness. In New York, a cab driver dreams of demons while awake. And a man who calls himself the Desolation Angel has returned to draw his old friends back to their hometown—a town where, two decades earlier, three boys committed the most brutal of rituals, an act of such intense savagery that it has ripped apart their minds. And where, in a cavern in a place called No Man's Land, something has been waiting a long time for those who stole something more precious than life itself.

___4695-4 $5.99 US/$6.99 CAN

Dorchester Publishing Co., Inc.
P.O. Box 6640
Wayne, PA 19087-8640

Please add $1.75 for shipping and handling for the first book and $.50 for each book thereafter. NY, NYC, and PA residents, please add appropriate sales tax. No cash, stamps, or C.O.D.s. All orders shipped within 6 weeks via postal service book rate. Canadian orders require $2.00 extra postage and must be paid in U.S. dollars through a U.S. banking facility.

Name_____
Address_____
City_____State_____Zip_____
I have enclosed $_____ in payment for the checked book(s).
Payment <u>must</u> accompany all orders. ❑ Please send a free catalog.

AMONG THE MISSING
RICHARD LAYMON

At 2:32 in the morning a Jaguar roars along a lonely road high in the California mountains. Behind the wheel sits a beautiful woman wearing only a skimpy nightgown. She's left her husband behind. She's after a different kind of man—someone as wild, daring, and passionate as herself. The man she wants is waiting patiently for her . . . with wild plans of his own. When the woman stops to pick him up, he suggests they go to the Bend, where the river widens and there's a soft, sandy beach. With the stars overhead and moonlight on the water, it's an ideal place for love. But there will be no love tonight. In the morning a naked body will be found at the Bend—a body missing more than its clothes. And the man will be waiting for someone else.

___4788-8 $5.99 US/$6.99 CAN

ONE RAINY NIGHT
RICHARD LAYMON

"If you've missed Laymon, you've missed a treat."
—Stephen King

The strange black rain falls like a shroud on the small town of Bixby. It comes down in torrents, warm and unnatural. And as it falls, the town changes. One by one, the inhabitants fall prey to its horrifying effect. One by one, they become filled with hate and rage . . . and the need to kill. Formerly friendly neighbors turn to crazed maniacs. A stranger at a gas station shoves a nozzle down a customer's throat and pulls the trigger. A soaking-wet line of movie-goers smashes its way into a theater to slaughter the people inside. A loving wife attacks her husband, still beating his head against the floor long after he's dead. As the rain falls, blood flows in the gutters—and terror runs through the streets.

"No one writes like Laymon, and you're going to have a good time with anything he writes."
—Dean Koontz

___4690-3 $5.99 US/$6.99 CAN

Dorchester Publishing Co., Inc.
P.O. Box 6640
Wayne, PA 19087-8640

Quenched

MARY ANN MITCHELL

An evil stalks the clubs and seedy hotels of San Francisco's shadowy underworld. It preys on the unfortunate, the outcasts, the misfits. It is an evil born of the eternal bloodlust of one of the undead, the infamous nobleman known to the ages as . . . the Marquis de Sade. He and his unholy offspring feed upon those who won't be missed, giving full vent to their dark desires and a thirst for blood that can never be sated. Yet while the Marquis amuses himself with the lives of his victims, with their pain and their torture, other vampires—of Sade's own creation—are struggling to adapt to their new lives of eternal night. And as the Marquis will soon learn, hatred and vengeance can be eternal as well—and can lead to terrors even the undead can barely imagine.

___4717-9 $5.50 US/$6.50 CAN

Dorchester Publishing Co., Inc.
P.O. Box 6640
Wayne, PA 19087-8640

Please add $1.75 for shipping and handling for the first book and $.50 for each book thereafter. NY, NYC, and PA residents, please add appropriate sales tax. No cash, stamps, or C.O.D.s. All orders shipped within 6 weeks via postal service book rate. Canadian orders require $2.00 extra postage and must be paid in U.S. dollars through a U.S. banking facility.

Name_____
Address_____
City_____ State_____ Zip_____
I have enclosed $_____ in payment for the checked book(s).
Payment <u>must</u> accompany all orders. ❑ Please send a free catalog.

. . . and coming
May 2001
from. . .

Elizabeth Massie
Wire Mesh Mothers

It all starts with the best of intentions. Kate McDolen, an elementary school teacher, knows she has to protect little eight-year-old Mistie from parents who are making her life a living hell. So Kate packs her bags, quietly picks up Mistie after school one day and sets off with her toward what she thinks will be a new life. How can she know she is driving headlong into a nightmare?

The nightmare begins when Tony jumps into the passenger seat of Kate's car, waving a gun. Tony is a dangerous girl, more dangerous than anyone could dream. She doesn't admire anything except violence and cruelty, and she has very different plans in mind for Kate and little Mistie. The cross-country trip that follows will turn into a one-way journey to fear, desperation . . . and madness.

___4869-8 $5.99 US/$6.99 CAN

The LOST

Jack Ketchum

It was the summer of 1965. Ray, Tim and Jennifer were just three teenage friends hanging out in the campgrounds, drinking a little. But Tim and Jennifer didn't know what their friend Ray had in mind. And if they'd known they wouldn't have thought he was serious. Then they saw what he did to the two girls at the neighboring campsite—and knew he was dead serious.

Four years later, the Sixties are drawing to a close. No one ever charged Ray with the murders in the campgrounds, but there is one cop determined to make him pay. Ray figures he is in the clear. Tim and Jennifer think the worst is behind them, that the horrors are all in the past. They are wrong. The worst is yet to come.

___4876-0 $5.99 US/$6.99 CAN